Into the Blue

Jody gazed down and the dark gleam of the dolphin's eye met her own. She *knew* this dolphin was as curious about her as she was about him. Her heart pounded with excitement.

The dolphin suddenly arced away from the boat, diving through the waves, then came racing back again, in a series of exhilarating leaps.

"Jody, we're waiting for you." It was her mother, standing in the hatchway.

Spray showered Jody as the dolphin darted away. "I'll be there in a minute," she called, and saw her mother go back inside.

Jody stood alone on the deck as the seconds ticked by, hoping the dolphin would return. But there was no sight or sound of her new friend. "Please come back tomorrow," she whispered.

Dolphin Diaries™

Ben M. Baglio

Illustrations by Judith Lawton

INTO THE BLUE

AN
APPLE
PAPERBACK

SCHOLASTIC INC.
New York Toronto London Auckland Sydney
Mexico City New Delhi Hong Kong Buenos Aires

ISBN 0-439-31947-1

12 11 10 9 8 1 2 3 4 5 6/0

Printed in the U.S.A. 40
First Scholastic printing, September 2001

Special thanks to Lisa Tuttle

1

June 19 — nearly midnight.

I'm so excited! Tomorrow morning the dream comes true; we set sail for the adventure of a lifetime. After more than two years of hoping and planning, Dolphin Universe is finally happening. A whole year of watching and following dolphins!

Jody McGrath put down her pen and began to play with the tiny silver dolphin that hung from a fine silver chain around her neck. Although she knew it was unscientific to be superstitious, she couldn't help feeling that this little ornament, a present from her Italian grandmother, had brought them all luck.

Her parents were marine biologists who had long dreamed of taking Jody and her twin brothers on an oceangoing yacht, to observe as many different kinds of dolphins as possible. Their idea was to sail from their home base in Florida, tracking and recording dolphins, and hooking up with other researchers around the world. But although many organizations were interested in contributing to the project, Craig and Gina McGrath had found it hard to raise the vast amount of money it would take to turn their dream into reality.

Then one day the little silver dolphin had arrived in the mail, with a note from Nonna saying: *To bring you luck*. On that very same day had come an offer from PetroCo, a major oil corporation, to provide the remainder of the money needed to go ahead with Dolphin Universe.

One of her father's favorite sayings came to mind: "There's no such thing as a free lunch." Jody's smile faltered. She picked up her diary again and paged back to find what she'd written then:

Of course, there's a catch. If we want PetroCo's money, we have to take their pet scientist along, too, a guy called Dr. Jefferson Taylor. It doesn't make any sense, since Mom and Dad are happy to share whatever they find. Mom says it's because businessmen don't understand how science works and only trust people they pay themselves. Dad says they just want to make themselves look good, and it's better to have another hand on deck than have to put advertisements on the sails and name the boat after the oil company! No way! There couldn't be a better name for our boat than "Dolphin Dreamer"!

Jody wondered what Dr. Jefferson Taylor was like. It was strange to think that, although she still hadn't met him, after tomorrow she would be seeing him every day. She and her younger brothers were already friends with the rest of the crew: their captain, Harry Pierce; first mate, Cameron Tucker; the cook/engineer, Mei Lin

Zhong; and especially Maddie, Craig and Gina's assistant. From the beginning of the project, Maddie had felt like family.

Jody knew that Dr. Taylor had only recently arrived in Florida from California, but she wondered why he hadn't come to the party her parents had given last week to celebrate the launch of Dolphin Universe.

"I don't think Dr. Taylor is much of a party animal," her father had commented dryly.

Jody had pounced. "You don't like him!"

"I didn't say that, Jo," her father replied.

"He's a well-respected researcher," her mother said. "Careful, methodical . . ."

"Fussy," concluded Craig McGrath. "He probably didn't come to the party in case he got onion dip on his suit."

"Give the guy a chance!" Gina protested.

But Jody had seen her mother biting her lip to keep from laughing.

Oh, well, she thought. If my parents can put up with Dr. Jefferson Taylor, so can I. He can't be any worse than my annoying twin brothers.

Jody looked at the poster on her bedroom wall. It showed three bottle-nosed dolphins rising high out of the deep blue ocean, caught by the photographer just as they were flying through the air. Jody thought it showed what she loved best about these animals: their grace, natural beauty, freedom, and playfulness. But although it was her favorite picture, she was leaving it behind. She wouldn't need it on the boat, with real dolphins so close at hand.

It was thoughts like these that made sleep impossible. Jody shivered with excitement, impatient for the night to pass. She picked up her diary again. She began to flip through it, remembering how much had happened in the past year: helping her parents outfit the boat, learning to sail and scuba dive, taking courses in first aid and lifesaving, all on top of her regular schoolwork, projects, and time spent with friends.

There were only two blank pages left. She was eager to start a new volume on board *Dolphin Dreamer*. Maybe by then she would already have met her first wild dolphins! The idea of keeping a "dolphin diary" had come from her father. He had told her many times about the summer he'd spent as a boy with his grandparents in Ireland, how he'd watched dolphins from the shore and kept a diary — which he'd shown her.

Jody had loved reading it. She had especially liked the sketches he had made of the dolphins and other wildlife. Craig McGrath could have been an artist if he hadn't become a scientist. A school project based on that diary had won a statewide competition, and Craig had gone on to study marine biology in college.

Jody had inherited her parents' fascination with dolphins. To her, there was nothing more interesting on earth than the playful, intelligent, mysterious creatures who belonged to the group of sea mammals called cetaceans. The chance to travel with her parents and share in their research really was a dream come true.

Of course it meant leaving school and her friends, but she would stay in touch with them via the Internet. And there would be no escaping schoolwork while they were at sea, no matter what her little brothers might think! One reason Craig and Gina McGrath had chosen Maddie out of all the graduate students who had applied for the job of their assistant was that she had trained as a schoolteacher and would be able to make sure that Jody and her brothers didn't fall behind in their studies.

But this was the start of summer vacation, with more than two months of glorious freedom stretching ahead! Jody was getting out of school a little early because of Dolphin Universe — her friends would still be stuck there for another week. She had said goodbye to them today, and they had promised to think of her tomorrow.

A soft knock at the door made her jump. The door opened and Gina McGrath poked her head in. "Oh, sweetheart, you're not still up?"

Jody smiled ruefully. "I can't sleep!"

Gina smiled back and came in with her arms outstretched. Jody jumped up and gave her mother a big, warm hug.

"I know how you feel," Gina said softly in her ear. "But try to get some rest. We've got a busy day tomorrow."

"Okay, I'll try," Jody replied. "Good night, Mom."

She climbed into bed and dutifully shut her eyes, as her mother put out the light.

* * *

The next thing Jody knew, Sean and Jimmy were marching through her room making enough noise for a small army as they whistled and shrieked and shouted, "D-Day, D-Day, D-Day!"

Dolphin Day!

For once Jody was too excited to get mad at them. Today of all days she didn't want to sleep in. She jumped up and rushed to get ready.

By nine o'clock the McGraths were at the marina just outside Fort Lauderdale. It was a beautiful day, already hot beneath the blazing sun, but with enough breeze to stir the rigging. Jody loved the familiar clanking sound made by the metal lines knocking against the masts.

She hurried along the narrow wooden jetties among the many boats of all sizes, her heart thumping with excitement as she caught sight of the elegant *Dolphin Dreamer*. She — for some reason, boats are always called "she" — was a beautiful two-masted schooner. The gleaming white fiberglass prow was decorated

Our home for the next year!

with a picture of two leaping dolphins, painted by Jody's father.

Of course, the twins were there first, swarming over the decks with bloodthirsty cries, pretending to be pirates. Jody felt like yelling with excitement herself, but she managed to quietly follow her parents.

"Those boys," sighed Gina. "I hope they'll calm down."

"If they don't, I'll drop 'em in the drink. That'll cool 'em off," Craig said, shifting the weight of his bags.

"They'd probably love it. They'd love to walk the plank," said Jody.

"A plank!" Her father winced comically. "I knew we'd forgotten something!"

Harry Pierce was waiting for them on deck. He was a tall, strongly built man with a weathered face and thick, closely cropped graying hair and beard. Jody had heard he was divorced and had a daughter her age who lived with her mother in West Palm Beach. Jody guessed that he must miss his daughter very much.

"Welcome aboard," Harry said, in his gruff English accent. He reached out to take Jody's bags. "We're all present and accounted for now."

"Dr. Taylor's arrived?" asked Gina, as she clambered nimbly aboard.

"He's getting settled in down below," Harry replied. Then he turned to Sean and Jimmy, bellowing, "Come on, boys! Look lively!" But his kind blue eyes were twinkling.

Sean and Jimmy responded immediately, rushing to stand at attention.

"Help your parents and get these things stowed below," Harry commanded.

"Aye, aye, sir!" Both boys spoke at once.

Jody stared in astonishment as her brothers each grabbed a bag and took it away without the slightest protest.

"They never obey me like that," Craig complained.

"Ah, but you're not the captain," said Harry with a wink. "I've explained the rules of the sea to them."

Jody carried her own bags belowdecks to her small two-bunked cabin. Her brothers were sharing an identical cabin next door, but Jody was lucky enough to have her cabin all to herself.

She spent some time busily unpacking and stashing things neatly away in the wall lockers. Though not normally so tidy — there were always far more interesting things to do with her time than putting things away —

Jody had been told that it was crucial to be tidy in the cramped confines of a boat. In an emergency, everyone on board had to be able to move swiftly and not be at risk of tripping over things. And in a storm, anything not properly stowed away could become a dangerous flying object.

When she'd managed to unpack everything, Jody emerged from her cabin eager to find out what was going on. She spotted Maddie standing in front of an open storage locker, checking off items against a clipboard.

Maddie, an attractive young African-American woman, was dressed in a white T-shirt and shorts that made her dark good looks even more striking.

"Have we got everything we need?" Jody asked.

Maddie grinned at her. "We've got everything on the list — if that's not everything we need, don't blame me!"

Passing through the main cabin, Jody paused to peek into the tiny kitchen — or galley, as it was called. She found the ship's cook putting away fruit, vegetables, and other fresh produce bought that morning. "Hi, Mei Lin," she called.

The small, slender Chinese woman turned. "Good

morning, Jody. You look happy. Your face is shining like the sun."

Jody felt her grin grow even broader. "Really? Well, I am happy. This has got to be the absolutely best day of my life!"

A small frown line appeared on Mei Lin's face and she murmured something in Chinese.

"What's that?" Jody asked curiously.

"Don't tempt fate," Mei Lin replied. "In China, it's very bad luck to talk too proudly. It attracts bad luck."

"Oh, that's just a superstition," Jody said. But she realized, as she spoke, that she was fingering the little silver dolphin at her neck as if it could keep her luck good.

"Jody!" Her mother was calling from the deck. "There's someone here to see you!"

"Oh, I'd better go. See you later, Mei!" Wondering who it could be, Jody scrambled up the stairs. As soon as she emerged, blinking against the blazing sun, she heard the sound of many hands clapping, and voices cheering, "Jo-dee, Jo-dee!"

Her heart gave a thump. She shaded her eyes and gazed up at the dock. Her jaw dropped in astonishment. There, in a long line, were all thirty-two of her classmates, and Mrs. Kilpatrick, her teacher.

Eager hands stretched out to help her cross from the boat to the dock, and a babble of voices broke out as everyone tried to say something to her at once.

"Quiet, class, please! One at a time!" Mrs. Kilpatrick's voice carried, calming them a little.

Jody's best friend, Lindsay, stepped out of line to hug her.

Jody thought now of how hard it was going to be not to see Lindsay every day, not to hear her voice on the phone whenever she wanted. "I'm really going to miss you," she said. Her voice squeaked a little at the end, and she swallowed hard.

"Me, too," whispered Lindsay. "Promise you'll e-mail me whatever you're thinking about, not just the website stuff that everybody can read."

Jody nodded. "You, too. Keep me up on what's happening."

"Here, I got you a going-away present." Smiling, Lindsay handed Jody a silver-wrapped rectangle. "Go on, open it."

Jody tore off the paper to find a book with a sky-blue cover embossed with a silver dolphin. There was no title; when she opened it, she discovered it was full of blank, lined pages. A new dolphin diary — much more special than the plain notebooks she'd bought to use on the trip. A lump in her throat made it impossible to speak. Shutting her eyes against the threatening tears, Jody hugged her friend again.

From behind her came the unmistakable whooping cries of Sean and Jimmy, while from the other direction came answering shrieks from their friends.

"Sounds like Mrs. Bacon's class has arrived," said Lindsay. She grimaced as the two boys raced past. "I don't envy you being trapped on that boat with the gruesome twosome."

"I don't envy myself, either," Jody agreed. "But Dad says the experience will make them more responsible. He says they'll surprise me. I'll let you know if they do!" She rolled her eyes at Lindsay, who responded with the same disbelieving look, and suddenly they were giggling helplessly as they hugged each other one last time.

More people were arriving at the marina to see the launch of *Dolphin Dreamer*: friends, sponsors, well-wishers, and reporters, including a camera crew from the local TV station WDOL. The station logo included a leaping dolphin, and it had been one of the earliest supporters of Dolphin Universe.

Melissa Myers, a glamorous reporter Jody had seen on television, was standing just a few feet away, carefully positioned so that the camera shot would include *Dolphin Dreamer* in the background as she spoke about this historic occasion. Then she gave Gina and Craig a chance to say a few words.

"Dolphins are fascinating and intelligent creatures," Craig began, gazing earnestly into the camera. "And we humans have always been very interested in them. My wife and I feel that the ideal way to study creatures of the sea is by living there, among them. Ideally, we'd have a submarine as well as a sailboat, but I'm afraid that, even with the generous sponsorship of PetroCo, our budget didn't quite stretch to that!"

Jody grinned. Around her, people were laughing appreciatively.

Gina McGrath took over the explanation. "We hope that we'll learn a lot by observing and recording the wild dolphins that we meet on our journey," she added. "But we're just as interested in the work that other people are doing, and we've scheduled visits all over the world with people who are studying or working with dolphins." Gina paused for Craig to continue.

"It's our plan to create a network among the 'dolphin people' of the world," Craig said. "Everything that we discover will go into a Dolphin Universe database. By sharing this information, we hope that not just scientists, but ordinary people will benefit. Anyone who is interested can visit our website."

Jody was so caught up in listening to her parents that she didn't realize that someone was talking to her until she felt a soft shove against her arm. Jody looked up in surprise to see a girl about her own age, taller than she was, with wavy, shoulder-length fair hair and a bad-tempered expression on an otherwise pretty face.

"I said, which one is Harry Pierce's yacht?" the girl repeated irritably. "Or don't you know, either?"

"Do you mean *Dolphin Dreamer*?" Jody asked.

"I don't know what the thing is called," the girl replied impatiently. "But Harry Pierce is the captain."

Jody pointed. "That's our boat, right there."

The girl gave a put-upon sigh. "I didn't ask about *your* boat. I want my *father*'s yacht — my father is Captain Harry Pierce."

"Oh! You're . . ." Jody searched her mind for the name of Harry's daughter. Brittany, that was it. "You're Brittany?" she asked. "Gosh, it's nice to meet you at last! I'm Jody McGrath — Harry works for my parents. It's their boat, actually . . ." Then, seeing the girl's frown deepen, she felt awkward. This prickly stranger wouldn't thank her for pointing out her mistake. Jody rushed on. "But you've come to the right place. Harry will be so pleased that you've come to say good-bye! I'll go tell him."

Brittany stared at Jody with distaste. "I didn't come to say good-bye," she snapped. "For your information, I'm sailing with my father to the Bahamas."

Jody couldn't believe what she was hearing. "But — you can't — I mean — look, somebody's made a mistake."

"Not me." Brittany raised her chin haughtily. "My mother doesn't make mistakes. She's very well organized. She would never have gone off to Paris without me if she hadn't arranged for me to have this vacation with my father. I would have rather gone to Paris, frankly, but she said I owe it to my father. He never spends any time with me. I've hardly seen him in two years. Anyway, it's only for a few weeks." She reached down and hoisted a designer-label carryall onto her shoulder.

Jody noticed she had two other bags as well.

"If you're not going to go and tell my father I'm here, you could at least help me carry something," Brittany said impatiently. "Or do you expect me to get all of this onto the boat by myself?"

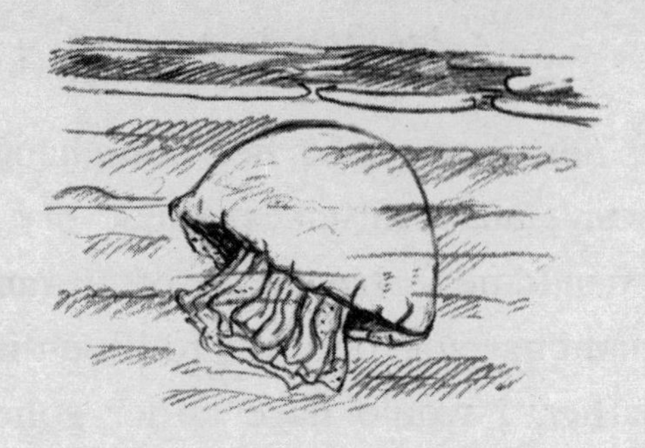

2

June 20 — 11:10 a.m.

It looks like I might have a new bunk mate. Her name is Brittany — and she's a pain in the neck! Harry seems to be phoning around half of Florida, trying to find someone who will look after his daughter — but so far, no luck.

Big surprise!

When she came on board, Brittany gave her father a letter. It was from Brittany's mother, saying sorry about the short notice, but she had to rush off to France (she didn't say why) and thought it would be great for Brittany and her father to spend some time together. She also said that Harry's description of his new job sounded like "an ideal learning experience" for Brittany.

All this was news to Brittany. She didn't know anything about Dolphin Universe. Her mother had just told her she was having a vacation in the Bahamas!

Harry said that his ex-wife must think that he could sail their daughter to the Bahamas anytime, no problem. But of course he can't — he's on Dolphin Dreamer *to do a job, like everyone else. And though* Dolphin Dreamer *will be stopping off at the Bahamas, it won't be for quite a while yet.*

Then Mom and Dad said that if push came to shove, one more passenger wouldn't cause any hardship, and there was even a spare bunk! No hardship? Maybe not for them, but that "spare" bunk just happens to be in my cabin!

But they're right, of course. It would be a disaster for Dolphin Universe if Harry had to pull out at the last minute to look after Brittany. Better to put up with some spoiled little rich girl for a few weeks than have to delay the whole journey. At least, I hope it will only be for a few weeks. . . .

Just heard Harry call to cast off. That's that, then. He mustn't have found anyone to take Brittany. We're off — and Brittany is coming with us.

Jody closed her diary, put it under her pillow, and rushed back up on deck. The press and some of the crowd were still there, cheering and whistling. Jody's school friends had said their final good-byes and returned to school earlier, but Brittany's arrival had delayed the scheduled departure time.

As Jody glanced at Brittany, she felt a pang of guilt for not wanting her around. Brittany's mother had lied to her daughter and left her. That was awful.

Jody decided to go over and try to make Brittany feel more welcome. But as she got closer, Jody could hear Brittany was still arguing with her father.

"Why can't you take me to the Bahamas *now*?" Brittany asked Harry yet again, as *Dolphin Dreamer* motored gently through the maze of the marina, toward the open sea.

Cameron Tucker had taken over the helm to allow the captain a chance to talk to his daughter. Maddie and Craig were standing by, waiting for the order to hoist the sails.

Jody decided to keep out of the way. She had been looking forward to this day for so long, and all she wanted to do was to enjoy it. But she couldn't help hearing every miserable word.

"Dr. McGrath said your schedule is flexible. You're not expected down in the Florida Keys for a week — or even more. Why can't we go to the Bahamas right now? Please, Daddy. *Please* . . ." Brittany's voice was sweet and wheedling.

"Brittany, what would be the point of that? Your mother isn't there, and I can't leave the boat and stay with you. I have a job to do, whatever you or your mother may think," her father replied. He was fidgeting and kept looking away, obviously deeply uncomfortable.

"I can stay in a hotel. I've got my own credit card, you know. Mommy wouldn't mind. I can look after myself!" Brittany said, proudly tossing back her long fair hair as she said it.

"Don't be ridiculous," Harry snapped. "You're only

thirteen." He took a deep breath, then spoke more calmly. "And I know your mother feels the same — if she thought you could look after yourself, she wouldn't have left you with me."

"I wish she hadn't!" Brittany cried.

So do we all, Jody thought. She gripped the side rail and stared at a passing boat being mobbed by a flock of seagulls.

Harry kept his temper. He didn't say what Jody was sure he was thinking, that he agreed with his daughter, too. Instead he spoke quietly, trying to calm her. "I only wish your mother had been honest with both of us when — "

"Mommy *was* honest with *me*!" Brittany interrupted. "She's always told the truth. *You're* the liar! You *could* take me to the Bahamas — you *could*! — *and* stay with me there. I don't know why you won't! You just don't want to — you've always been horrible to me!" Jody thought she sounded near to tears.

"Brittany — " Her father sounded concerned now.

"Leave me *alone*!" With that finally shouted word, Brittany vanished belowdecks.

Her father stood there for a few seconds, then turned to walk slowly in Jody's direction. Jody saw that the captain, usually so calm and certain, looked upset.

Harry spotted her then, and his weather-beaten face went a shade redder. "Did you hear all that?" he sighed.

Jody blushed, too, and nodded.

"I hope she'll settle down," Harry said. "Of course, it's hard for her — she must be feeling let down by her mother. But most kids would love a chance to spend the summer sailing on *Dolphin Dreamer* — don't you think so?" he asked anxiously.

"I can't think of anything better," Jody said honestly.

He nodded, still uncertain. "I'd always hoped my daughter would like sailing. I wanted to teach her when she was younger, but her mother could never see the point of it." He sighed again, shook his head, and moved away.

Jody went to join her brothers, who were leaning over the side, too busy talking to each other to have noticed the argument. "What're you looking at?" she asked.

"Jellyfish!" they both shouted.

Jody looked down into the frothy water where a Portuguese man-of-war floated like a pink, crested football. Three other smaller ones clustered nearby. She was suddenly aware of silence: The drone of the engine had stopped.

"Ready!" called Cam.

With a flap and a sound like a sudden, deep breath, the sails caught the wind and filled. They were sailing! Jody listened to the slap of waves against the side of the boat, and felt the sun's heat on her bare arms. She leaned out into the wind, breathing in the fresh, salty tang of the air, and narrowed her eyes against the sun's glare.

The marina and the traffic around it were receding, and already the land seemed far away. Jody felt as if she had entered another world where petty problems — like Brittany's bad temper — didn't matter. She sighed deeply. The ocean was working its magic. If Brittany would come out, instead of lurking below, she would feel it, too. She was bound to cheer up and act better, Jody thought optimistically.

She looked around at the others. Harry had taken over at the helm, looking more relaxed in his role as captain than he had as Brittany's father. Jody's own father was discussing something with Maddie, while Cam, who stood nearby, was gazing at her with a wistful expression on his face.

Gina was rubbing sunscreen onto Sean's freckled face, while Jimmy waited his turn. The twins were redheaded and fair-skinned like their father, which meant they had to take extra care in the sun. Jody thought she was lucky to have inherited her mother's Mediterranean complexion, which tanned instead of burned.

Everyone was on deck except Mei Lin, Brittany, and Dr. Jefferson Taylor. Jody still hadn't met their new crew member. In the uproar surrounding Brittany's unexpected arrival she had forgotten all about him. She wondered where he was.

Just then, like an answer to her question, a pinkish, balding head poked up out of the hold, reminding her of a turtle coming out of its shell. After a cautious look around, the owner of the head emerged onto the deck. He was middle-aged and overweight, puffing a little, as if even pulling himself up the few steps was more exercise than he was used to. Dark glasses hid his eyes, and he was smartly dressed in a navy-blue short-sleeved shirt, white trousers, and expensive deck shoes.

"Dr. Taylor," Gina called. "Please come and join us. Can I offer you some sunscreen?"

Jefferson Taylor gazed around and touched the top of his bare head. "I can tell that I'll need a hat."

"Yes, a hat is a good idea if you're going to be in the sun for very long," Gina replied. "But you could sit there, by Jody, in the shade. I don't think you've met my children yet, have you? That's my daughter, Jody, and these two are Sean and Jimmy."

Dr. Taylor nodded rather stiffly. "Pleased to meet you, Jody. And you . . . er . . . boys."

"I'll bet you can't tell us apart," crowed Jimmy.

"I don't approve of betting," Dr. Taylor said rather primly. "However, I am a scientist, and the essence of science is observation." He whipped off his dark glasses, revealing a pair of brown eyes with surprisingly long, thick lashes. He thrust his head forward, right into the twins' faces, making Sean flinch, although Jimmy held his ground and stared back.

Dr. Taylor just looked, silent and unblinking, for several long seconds. "As I thought," he said. "There are distinct differences in the freckle pattern. Anyone who cared to look closely could tell you apart. Easy to miss at a distance, of course. I suspect behavioral differences would be of more practical use."

"What does that mean?" demanded Jimmy.

"In this case I would guess that you, Sean, are slightly more cautious. And you, Jimmy, are the troublemaker!" Dr. Taylor emphasized his words by pointing his stubby forefinger.

Gina burst out laughing. "You've got that one right!"

Dr. Taylor smiled, replaced his dark glasses, and turned away. "Of course. Now, if you'll excuse me, I'm going to get my hat."

The boys stared after him, mouths open. Jody couldn't hold it back any longer and began to giggle uncontrollably.

"Differences in the freckle pattern," Gina murmured, and then she began to laugh again. "Maybe we should call them Spotty and Splotch?" She leaned against Jody, and they both giggled hysterically as the two boys scowled.

Jody leaned over the side of the boat and gazed at the seemingly endless expanse of flat blue water. Almost two hours had gone by, they were well out to sea, and she had yet to see a single dolphin. She felt bored and disappointed.

It just didn't seem possible. More often than not when she'd gone sailing with her parents they'd seen dolphins. Sometimes it was just a leaping figure in the distance, but often they would swim right up to the boat. They weren't shy creatures and there were lots of them in the coastal waters around Florida — where they were now. So where were they all?

"You know what they say about a watched pot?" Jody turned to find her mother smiling at her sympathetically.

Jody sighed. "They say it never boils — but that's not true. The water will boil when it gets hot enough, no matter how many people are watching."

"Ooh, that sounds like a scientific observation worthy of Dr. Jefferson Taylor!" Gina McGrath's dark eyes twinkled with mischief.

Jody couldn't help laughing. "It's just so frustrating! I've been looking forward to this day for so long, and . . ." She shrugged, unable to find the words to express her disappointment.

Jody saw that her mother understood.

"I know, sweetie," Gina said. "We all feel the same. Luckily, we've got as much time as it takes for the dolphins to find us. It's a funny thing, but I've found that when you're looking hardest for dolphins is when you don't find them. It's when you're thinking about something else that they suddenly pop up. So why don't you think about something else . . . like the skyscraper of sandwiches that Mei Lin is putting together down in the galley? If we don't start eating, we're going to have a storage problem!"

As soon as her mother mentioned the word "sandwiches," Jody realized how hungry she was. "Well, you can count on me to help!"

Gina touched her shoulder. "What would really be helpful would be for you to go tell Brittany it's time for lunch."

Jody's heart sank. "Sure," she agreed.

Jody felt apprehensive as she turned away. She hoped the other girl would have cooled down by now, but it seemed like a bad sign that she was still sulking in their cabin rather than coming out and trying to make friends.

Jody made herself sound cheerful as she breezed in. "Hi, Brittany, Mom says — "

"Don't you believe in knocking?" Brittany, huddled in a corner of one of the bunks, glared angrily.

"Not on the door of my own cabin," Jody said, frowning.

Brittany groaned. "Oh, that's just perfect — I have to share a room!"

"Yeah, I was pretty thrilled when you turned up, too." As Jody spoke, she saw how red Brittany's eyes and nose were, and realized she must have been crying. She felt ashamed of herself for sniping at the poor girl. It must be awful to feel nobody wanted you. "I just came to tell you it's lunchtime." Jody spoke gently now. "Why don't we take our sandwiches on deck? Maybe we'll get lucky and see some dolphins."

Brittany snorted. "What is it with dolphins all the time?"

"Didn't your dad explain?" Jody asked.

Brittany shrugged. "About your parents' job, yeah. I know they study dolphins, and they're going to be traveling around the world meeting other people who study dolphins, and gathering all the information together and stuff like that. Boring! Why should I care about it? *My* dad's a sailor, but that doesn't mean I have to like being stuck on a boat for weeks and weeks!" Her eyes glittered with the threat of more tears.

Jody sighed. "Fair enough," she said. "But I love dolphins because they're wonderful, not just because my parents study them for a living. I'm part of Dolphin Universe, too. I've been working to help make it happen for more than a year." She leaned forward, eager to make Brittany understand.

But the other girl only snorted again. "You're just a kid — I'll bet you're younger than me."

"I'm twelve — the same age my father was when he first started studying dolphins," Jody defended herself. "He says — "

"Oh, who cares," said Brittany abruptly, getting to her feet. "Did you say it was lunchtime? I'm starving."

Brittany's rudeness smarted, but Jody tried not to mind. When they reached the galley, she introduced Mei Lin to Brittany. "Mei's our cook and chief engineer."

"That sounds like a weird combination," Brittany said, her mouth twisting with scorn.

"Well, I was an engineering student back in Beijing," Mei Lin explained patiently. "But when I came to America, I couldn't afford to continue my studies. My English was terrible then, too," she added, making a face. "But better now," she smiled, as she began to slice a loaf of bread into thin, even slices.

She continued her story. "First, I got a job as a cook at the marina, where I got to know Harry. But I was always helping people fix their cars and, as word got around, people asked me to fix their boats, too. Then Harry came into the marina one day and told me about this job. I thought it sounded like fun!"

Mei Lin looked down at the pile of buttered bread in front of her. "What kind of sandwiches would you like? Tuna, cheese, ham, or peanut butter and jelly?"

Brittany seemed to relax at Mei Lin's soft manner. She asked for tuna, even giving the cook a quick smile as she thanked her.

Jody and Brittany took their tuna sandwiches and large plastic cups full of iced tea onto the deck. The afternoon was hot and still. The boat did not seem to be moving at all. Cam was at the helm, a bored expression on his face.

"Any dolphins yet?" Jody asked him.

"Nope." Cam shrugged his broad shoulders.

"Have you tried knocking on the side?" Jody asked. Then she added for Brittany's benefit, "Dolphins are attracted by sound, so if there are any in the area they might come over to see what the noise was about."

Cam grinned, his even teeth brilliantly white in his tanned, handsome face. "Oh, I leave all that technical stuff to the experts, you and your parents. Harry just hired me to help him sail the boat — even when there's not a breath of wind."

"Why don't you use the motor?" Brittany asked.

"No point wasting fuel," Cam said. "It's a mighty big ocean, and we're not exactly going anywhere anyway."

Brittany frowned. "What do you mean, we're not going anywhere?"

"Jody could probably explain that better than me," he said.

Jody felt her stomach clench nervously as Brittany looked at her. She remembered Brittany's argument with her father that morning, and didn't want to stir it up again. She tried to change the subject. "Cam, aren't you having lunch?"

"I'm okay, Jody, thanks. Maddie's bringing me something." Cam gave her a wink.

"What did he mean, Jody?" Brittany demanded.

"Just that we're not going straight to a place," Jody replied. "We're looking for dolphins. If we find a group of dolphins we'll probably follow them for a while."

"And if we don't?" Brittany glared at Jody as if she had her to blame for her troubles.

"Oh, we're bound to!" A high, wailing cry made Jody break off and look up. She saw a flock of seagulls overhead, calling to one another. One flew very low, nearly brushing her head with its wings, and Jody ducked.

Brittany laughed. "That bird doesn't seem to like you," she said.

"I think it wants food," Jody replied. She tore off a bit of crust and tossed it into the air. Immediately a shrieking, midair bird battle erupted.

"You shouldn't have done that," Cam said. "Now they'll *never* leave us alone!"

Three birds landed in a row on the side of the boat, very close to the girls. They stretched their necks, turned their heads, and peered at Jody and Brittany with bright, greedy eyes. Three or four other birds swooped overhead.

Cam stood up and waved his arms aggressively. "Go on, get outta here, shoo!"

The seagulls on the side left their perch, but their places were immediately taken by others.

"Eat up quickly," Cam advised. "Those greedy birds won't leave until there's not a scrap of food left in sight."

"I'm going inside," said Brittany, and left.

Feeling a little foolish, Jody wolfed down her sandwich.

"One ham on rye with mustard, and a pickle on the side," Maddie sang out, emerging from below. She held a blue plastic plate high above her head, balanced on the palm of one hand like a truck-stop waitress.

Jody opened her mouth to warn her about the birds, but it was already too late. Seeing its chance, the nearest gull left its perch and swooped on the sandwich, seizing one corner and flapping away with the top slice of bread. Shrieking angrily, the others followed it into the sky, all struggling for a share.

Maddie stared after them, openmouthed. She had only just managed to keep hold of the plate. "Well," she said. "That's one they never warned us about in waitress school! How do you feel about an open-faced sandwich?"

Cam laughed and took the plate to examine the leavings. "Fine — if I get a chance to eat it! Maybe I'd better go below for my lunch . . . if you ladies wouldn't mind taking the helm?"

"Oh, I think I could probably manage on my own at *this* speed," said Maddie, taking his place.

The seagulls returned to circle the boat briefly but, sensing there was nothing else to steal, they soon flew away.

The rest of the day passed slowly and uneventfully. Jody even found herself yawning, tempted by sleep in the peaceful heat of the day, but she was determined not to give up her dolphin watch. The thought of another encounter with Brittany also kept her on deck until Harry finally announced that, as there was so little wind, they might as well take in the sails and put down the anchor for the night.

Jody was disappointed that her first day of dolphin-watching hadn't been more of a success, but dinner was soon announced and she went below to join the others.

Mei Lin had made tagliatelle bolognese. "In honor of Dr. Gina," she said.

Craig pretended to be miffed. "What about honoring the Irish side of the family?"

The cook looked worried, obviously not realizing he was teasing. "Oh, Dr. Craig! Please excuse me! I understand what is Italian cooking. But I don't understand what is Irish cooking — "

"Mei, I was only teasing," said Craig. "This is a wonderful meal."

"But I am serious," Mei said. "I would like to learn how to cook Irish food."

"In that case, you'll have to find somebody else to teach you, because I'm the Microwave Man," Craig said with a grin.

"Shall we have some music?" suggested Harry as everyone started eating. He hovered over the CD collection that had made up a major part of his luggage. "In keeping with the Italian theme of the evening, I suggest *La Traviata*."

"Oh, Daddy, not one of those awful operas! It's not even sung in English!" moaned Brittany.

"You don't have to understand the words to enjoy the music," Harry said firmly.

Jody paused with her fork halfway to her mouth as the captain's mention of music triggered a memory.

She knew that the Ancient Greeks had discovered that dolphins had a love for music. She had read a story once about dolphins being attracted by the playing of flutes. And for the past year at school she had been learning to play the recorder, an old-fashioned wind instrument a little like a flute.

All of those thoughts came together to give Jody a brilliant idea, and she couldn't wait to try it out. "May I please be excused?"

Her mother looked at her, surprised. "There's still dessert to come."

"I know, but there's something I want to do before it gets dark," Jody replied. She looked pleadingly at her mother, who nodded permission.

Jody dashed back to her cabin and dug out her recorder, then hurried up on deck.

Outside, the sun had set, but there was still light in the sky. It was twilight, that hazy, blue hour that was Jody's favorite time of day. It was when the air seemed most like water, when she could imagine herself diving upward into it, to fly as easily as swimming. Away from the noise and artificial lights of the land, the atmosphere was peaceful and dreamlike, a time and place where wishes could come true.

Jody settled down, cross-legged, on the foredeck and raised the recorder to her lips. She played the first tune she'd learned and then stopped, peering out at the water for some response. Nothing. She tried "Greensleeves." Then the "Skye Boat Song." Still nothing.

Jody decided to tackle something a bit more difficult — one of the classical pieces her teacher had given her to work on while she was away. She didn't want to go below for the sheet music, so she played from memory. It was a struggle to get the notes right. When she made a mistake, she started over again. Then again.

She was concentrating so hard on the music that she forgot all about her reason for playing it. Utterly absorbed, she came to the end and as she was sitting quietly, the silence was suddenly broken by a sound like a squeaky door hinge.

Jody caught her breath. The gentle creaking noise came again, rising in pitch, almost like a question. She stood up and leaned over the starboard bow, straining her eyes to see. Nearly all the light had drained out of the day by now, and although she thought she saw a dark shape in the water, she couldn't be absolutely sure — until it leaped straight out of the water, and she saw the unmistakable curving bulk of a dolphin, so close she could almost have reached out and touched it.

As it went under, a spray of seawater showered her. Jody laughed with delight. The dolphin poked its head up. It seemed to be smiling at her. Jody knew this was just the shape of the beak and mouth — all bottle-nosed dolphins look as if they're smiling, even when they're unhappy. All the same, she felt this one really *was* happy. She couldn't help feeling it was as pleased as she was by this encounter.

"Did you like the music?" she asked. "I was playing it for you. Do you want some more?"

The dolphin responded with a whistle followed by a series of rapid clicks and pops.

"Okay." Jody raised her recorder to her lips and played the passage she had struggled with before. This time, it came out perfectly.

When she'd finished, there was a moment of silence. Jody gazed down and the dark gleam of the dolphin's eye met her own. She felt a shock of connection. She *knew* this dolphin was as curious about her as she was about him. Her heart pounded with excitement.

The dolphin suddenly arced away from the boat, diving through the waves.

"Oh, don't go!" Jody cried. But as soon as she spoke, she realized her new friend wasn't leaving at all. He

Dancing Dolphin

came racing back again, expressing his happiness through speed and a series of exhilarating leaps. Jody felt like doing the same thing. She wanted to jump right into the water with him.

"Jody, we're waiting for you. Don't you want dessert?" It was her mother, standing in the hatchway.

"Mom, there's a dolphin here!" Jody called back excitedly.

Spray showered her as he darted away.

"It's too dark to see," Gina objected.

Jody held her breath, listening for the sound of the dolphin — but he had vanished into the night.

"Come in now, Jo. Time to look for dolphins again after the sun comes up," her mother said firmly.

"I'll be there in a minute," Jody called, and saw her mother go back inside.

The seconds ticked by as Jody stood alone on the deck, hoping the dolphin would return. But there was no sight or sound of her new friend.

"Please come back tomorrow," she whispered, and then, full of excitement and hope for the morning, she went below.

June 20 — bedtime.

My first sighting!

1. Bottle-nosed Dolphin (Tursiops truncatus)

Dark gray, with lighter gray underside. No obvious markings or scars noticed. Age unknown (Dad thinks fairly young, probably over four — since otherwise he'd be traveling with his mother's group — but under ten). Sex unknown (but I think he's a male).

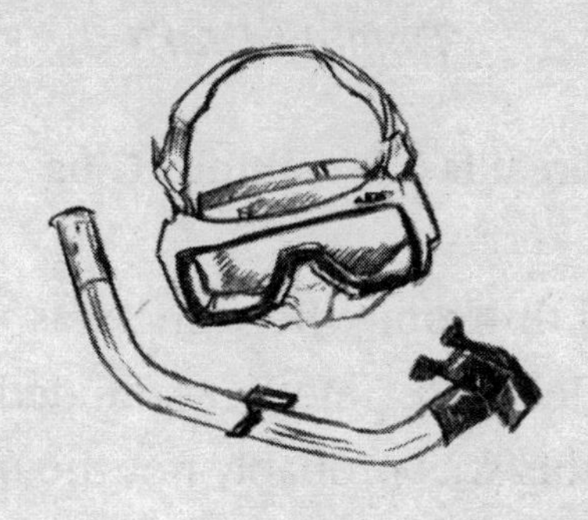

3

June 21 — 8 a.m.

He was still there this morning. I came up on deck first thing to see, and he was swimming around the boat. When he saw me, he came right up out of the water and practically stood on his tail. It was the weirdest thing — it felt like he had been looking for me and was really excited to find that I hadn't disappeared overnight. Wouldn't it be funny if he's studying us, just like we're studying him? Maybe when he gets back to his pod they'll be talking about "Human Universe" and complaining about how hard it is to study creatures that have to stay on dry land and almost never get into the water.

"Jody, your breakfast is waiting," Gina called from the hatchway.

Jody looked up from where she was writing in her diary on the deck. Her mother sounded exasperated. Jody realized this was probably not the first time she'd been called. Still, she couldn't pull herself away from the fascination of her new friend. "Mom, there's a dolphin here," she explained.

Gina joined her daughter and gazed down at the dolphin who was swimming in lazy circles just off the port bow. "How many are there?" she asked.

"Just this one," Jody replied. "He was here last night." She couldn't stop smiling.

"And no sign of any others?" Gina asked. "That's odd. Dolphins nearly always travel in groups, even if they're very small ones. You don't often meet lone dolphins, especially not away from a harbor."

"Isn't he great?" Jody sighed happily.

Gina pursed her lips thoughtfully. "I wonder how he'd respond if one of us got into the water."

Jody caught her breath with excitement. "Oh, Mom, could I?"

"I meant me, honey," Gina replied. She bit her lip ruefully. "I'm sorry, but this seems like a good opportunity to check out the camera and get some footage off to WDOL. Then if there are any glitches we should be able to straighten them out before we sail too far away from Florida."

Jody wasn't giving up just yet. "Okay, but I could come in *with* you, couldn't I?" she said eagerly. She had received her junior scuba diving certificate three months earlier and couldn't wait to use her new skill. "I promise I won't get in the way, and —"

"Another time." Her mother sounded firm.

"But why?" Jody tried not to whine, but it was so disappointing.

"Several reasons," her mother replied briskly. She ticked them off on her fingers. "One, we might scare him off. Lone dolphins are usually fine with lone swimmers, but two might seem too many. Two, although dolphins aren't known to be aggressive toward people, there have been the occasional incidents when people have gotten hurt. Remember, this is a wild animal. Three, accidents can happen, and even though you know how to handle yourself in the water, I'd be tempted to keep an eye on you when I need to concentrate on my work."

Jody sighed and gave in to the inevitable. "Okay."

"You'll have your chance soon," Gina promised. "Now, come down and have something to eat."

Everyone was enthusiastic about Gina's plan — everyone, that was, except Brittany.

Her eyes narrowed and her face tightened with displeasure. "You mean we're just going to sit here while Dr. McGrath takes pictures of some fish?"

"It's a dolphin, Brittany," Jody corrected her. "Dolphins are mammals, not fish."

"I don't care what it is," Brittany snapped rudely. "I thought we were supposed to be sailing to Key West, then going on to the Bahamas. What is the deal? If it doesn't matter where we are, why don't we just go to the Bahamas now? There must be loads of dolphins there."

Her father, who was sipping a second cup of coffee, frowned, then said slowly and clearly, "Brittany, I've already explained to you. *Dolphin Dreamer* is not your private pleasure cruiser. This is a scientific expedition, and our schedule is set by the scientists, not a spoiled teenager."

Brittany jumped up from her seat. "Thanks a lot," she shouted. "I never asked to come with you. I don't want to be here. So why don't you just drop me off somewhere . . . anywhere . . . the sooner the better!"

Jody saw Harry clench his jaw tensely, then take a deep breath and relax his face again. "Brittany, you know very well why not," he said calmly. "I hope we're not going to have to go through this every day. The sooner you accept the situation and make the best of it, the better."

"The sooner I get away from you, the better!" Brittany cried. "I want to go home!" Then she burst into tears and stumbled out of the main cabin in the direction of her cabin.

There was an embarrassed silence.

Finally, Harry Pierce spoke. "I'm sorry about that," he said. "Brittany's had a bit of a rough time what with her mother and me splitting up. . . ." He waved a hand vaguely, looking miserable.

"Have you been able to get in touch with Brittany's mother?" Gina asked, her voice gentle.

Harry shook his head. "Her cell phone is still switched off. Maybe she didn't take it with her. I've left an urgent message for her at the hotel in Paris where she usually stays, and also a long e-mail explaining how impossible this situation is for all of us. I'm sure she'll be in touch very soon, to make some other arrangements, but in the meantime . . . I'm afraid you're stuck with Brittany."

"You mean she's stuck with us," said Craig gently. "Life will be easier for us all if we can convince her that we're really not so bad. Jody, you'll have to be our goodwill ambassador. Try to make friends with her."

Jody nodded unhappily, wondering how to get through to somebody who wouldn't listen, somebody who didn't care about anything she found interesting, and who had made it clear she didn't like her.

"Now let's get this show on the road," said Craig briskly, and the mood in the room changed to one of excitement.

Up on deck, Gina pulled on a wetsuit. Although the water was warm, it would protect her from jellyfish stings and other potential hazards. While Jody watched, wishing she was the one suiting up, Craig helped her mother fit on her weight belt, buoyancy vest, and dive computer.

Craig then checked the air gauge. "You've got a full tank, but let's keep this first time down shallow and short," he suggested. "Half an hour okay?"

"Sure." Gina grinned, putting fins on her feet. "I don't want to wear out my welcome with our finny friend."

Maddie was lowering the hydrophone — an underwater microphone — over the side of the boat into the water. The object was to record dolphin sounds, but the hydrophone often picked up lots more. Jody had been surprised to learn that the underwater world was far from silent; a lot of fish made noises.

Cameron emerged from the hatchway carrying the video monitor. "Where d'you want this, boss?" he asked Craig.

Gina arched an eyebrow. "You're going to be watching what I film on deck?"

"Naw, there's a Miami Dolphins game I want to see," Craig said, straight-faced.

Jody giggled and Gina laughed, too. "Well, I hope we don't find out the hard way that the monitor's not as waterproof as the camera!"

Harry glanced at the small flags called telltales fluttering in the breeze, and then peered over the side where the water was growing choppier. "Wish we'd had a bit of this wind yesterday," he said. "But you'll be all right."

"Just don't splash too much," said Craig. "I hate being disturbed when I'm watching football."

Gina made a face at him, then fitted her mask snugly on her face and put the air regulator into her mouth. She entered the water with a great stride off the dive platform. Then, when Gina had signaled that she was okay, Maddie handed her the camera, in its bright yellow waterproof housing.

Jody's heart pounded with excitement as she leaned over the edge and watched her mother's gentle descent below the surface. Sean and Jimmy jostled for position beside her, but Jody hardly noticed. She was watching the silvery stream of bubbles rising up as her mother sank lower. In her mind, she, too, had left the surface for the beautiful, mysterious underwater world. But the way the sunlight hit the waves, and the darkness of the deeper water, made it hard to follow her mother's progress. As Gina descended farther, she became a murky figure to Jody. Jody could follow the rising stream of bubbles only with her eyes, focus on the bright yellow case of the camera, and try to imagine her mother's movements.

Jody gazed around in search of the dolphin, wondering what he would make of this visitor to his world. He had been cruising in gentle arcs around *Dolphin Dreamer* all morning, only occasionally zooming off at a high speed. Jody wondered if he was inviting them to give chase for a game of tag. Dolphins were known to be playful creatures. But where was he now? Then she saw the large, smooth, streamlined shape of the dolphin streaking along beneath the surface, heading straight for Gina.

Jody caught her breath, suddenly nervous. It was such a big animal! Seeing it approaching her mother, she knew that all it would take was a careless switch of the tail, or an accidental bump, for damage to be done. If the air regulator got pulled out of Gina's mouth, or if she were knocked unconscious, she'd be in serious trouble.

But just as it seemed that the dolphin was about to hit Gina, he veered away, shooting past her with a simple flex of his powerful body. Jody let out a relieved breath, seeing that there had never been anything to worry about. The dolphin had been in total control. It must have known to the inch — or less — how close he could come without actually touching his visitor.

"Echolocation, remember?" said her dad, as if he'd read her mind. "Even in deep, murky water, dolphins don't bump into things."

Jody nodded.

"Echo-what?" said Sean, frowning.

"Echolocation," Craig repeated, smiling. "It means finding out where things are by using sound instead of sight."

Sean still looked confused.

Their father explained further. "Dolphins find their way by making a sound that bounces off objects around them and comes back to the dolphin as an echo. From hearing this *echo* the dolphin knows the *location* of whatever the sound waves have hit."

"I get it," said Jimmy, nodding. "It's like bats using radar."

"Cool," said Sean. But he still looked puzzled. "Are dolphins *blind*?"

"Oh, no," said Craig. "It's just that sound is more useful to them underwater — but they can see all right! Have a look at that one, eyeing your mother!"

Jody gazed down into the water to where her mother was hovering, kicking her fins against the currents to stay in roughly one place as she aimed the camera at the dolphin.

He was watching her with what looked like friendly interest, lying horizontally in the water, barely moving; facing Gina at first, then turning to lie on one side and gaze at her with one eye.

Jody wished she could get a better view, but with the

wind chopping the surface, and her mother following the dolphin farther away from the side of the boat, it was hard to see anything in detail.

"Hey, kids, you ought to come see this — your mom's getting some great pictures!"

At their father's call, Jody, Sean, and Jimmy all left their spots at the side to watch on the monitor instead.

The dolphin's head almost filled the screen as he seemed to smile directly into the camera. Jody caught her breath in wonder. Her mother must be so close to him! Close enough to touch . . .

As she thought this, the dolphin loomed larger as the camera drew even closer, and then Gina's hand came into view. Jody held her breath, watching as the hand reached for the animal, but before contact could be made, the dolphin slipped away. He didn't go far. He might not be willing to be touched, but he was obviously too curious about Gina to leave.

The dolphin circled, then rolled on his side. Then he rose up until he appeared to be standing on his tail. Jody wondered if he was imitating Gina's upright, two-legged stance. It was annoying not to be able to see everything. She wished she could be there, underwater, alongside her mother.

"It would be more interesting if we could see Mom, too, and know what the dolphin was reacting to," she said. "Somebody else should be underwater with them."

"And I think I know who you think that somebody

Mom meets Apollo

should be," her father said teasingly. He patted her shoulder. "You'll get your chance, honey, don't worry. I didn't pay for your scuba diving lessons for nothing!"

Dr. Taylor had been standing back, just watching without comment. Now he said in his rather formal way, "May I ask what you are hoping to learn by this exercise?"

"Excuse me?" said Craig.

"Why is Dr. McGrath filming this particular dolphin?" Dr. Taylor asked.

"Because it's there," Craig said jokingly. Then, with an expression almost as solemn as Jefferson Taylor's round, moonlike face, he went on. "I'm sorry, I didn't mean to be flippant, but didn't you read the Dolphin Universe prospectus? We are here to record our observations on all the dolphins we come across. Our video footage, still photos, and sound recordings will then form a database, which will be available to all interested researchers."

Dr. Taylor rubbed his chin. "Ah, yes . . ." He seemed

to be thinking hard. "Er, I will be conducting research, too, while we're at sea, of course. PetroCo will expect me to contribute something special. Yes, indeed . . ." Nodding to himself, the scientist wandered away.

Jody saw her father roll his eyes, and she was sure that Maddie was hiding a grin as she bent to turn up the sound on the hydrophone.

Although the meeting between her mother and the dolphin had appeared to be silent from Jody's position above, now she could hear a steady stream of low clicks and occasional high-pitched squeaks. These sounds wouldn't carry into the air above, but no doubt her mother would hear them in the water.

All too soon, the half hour was over, and Gina returned slowly to the surface. The dolphin followed, poking his head up through the waves and whistling at her.

Pulling away her mouthpiece, Gina spoke to the dolphin, "Don't worry, you haven't seen the last of me!" She handed the camera to Craig, and the twins stretched out eager hands to help by taking her fins before she climbed up the ladder back onto the boat. "I could have stayed down a lot longer, you know," she said wistfully.

"Sometimes I think you were a dolphin in a previous life," Craig teased.

"This wind is too good to miss," said Harry. "Do you need to stay here any longer, or can we get under sail?"

"That's fine with me," said Gina.

Craig nodded at the video equipment. "Just let us get this stuff down below. Maddie, we'd better pull in the hydrophone, too, if we're going to be traveling at any speed." He turned back to his wife. "The picture's beautifully clear. Wait'll you see it."

Jody hung over the side and gazed at the dolphin. He seemed to be still waiting for something. "That was my mom," she said. "Next time it'll be me, I promise." She turned, tensing as she saw Brittany come lurching onto the deck.

"I feel awful," the girl groaned to her father. She looked pale, almost greenish. "Can't you make the boat lie still?"

"It'll feel smoother once we're actually sailing, love,"

Harry promised her. "We'll get going soon. . . . Wait! Where are you going?" he called, as Brittany stumbled away again.

"Back to my cabin to lie down," Brittany replied.

"You'll feel worse if you go below," he warned her. "Honestly, love, the best thing if you're feeling seasick is to stay on deck, in the fresh air."

"You'd better not be making that up," Brittany muttered.

Jody decided she didn't want to be around if Brittany was going to keep complaining or start being sick. With one more fond look at the friendly dolphin, she went below.

She found her parents in the main cabin with Dr. Taylor and Maddie, getting ready to review the video.

"There, look, he's mimicking my posture," Gina said. "Now, you'll see the camera angle change . . . that's because I rolled onto my front to see if he'd do the same — and he did. He was great. Even though he wouldn't let me touch him, he was really interacting with me."

"We should think of a name for him," said Jody.

Dr. Taylor looked surprised. "Oh, surely not?" he said.

"What's wrong with that?" demanded Gina. "It's a good suggestion."

"Well, people name their pets," Dr. Taylor replied, "but that animal is not a pet. If you give it a name, you'll start imagining that it has a personality. Very unscientific."

"I'm sorry, Dr. Taylor, I have to disagree," Gina said. "Scientists who study animals often give them names."

Despite her mother's careful tone, Jody could tell that Gina was annoyed.

"It makes it easier to talk about them without confusion," Gina continued. "I know we're only talking about one dolphin now, but in a few days —"

"But surely numbers would do just as well for identification and wouldn't encourage the wrong attitude toward the dolphins," Dr. Taylor argued heatedly. "They are scientific subjects to us, after all. They're not our friends."

Now it was Jody's turn to disagree. "As far as I'm concerned, dolphins *can* be friends."

"Personally, I've always liked names better than numbers, and most people find them easier to remember," said Craig easily.

Jody smiled gratefully at her father.

"And I think Jody should choose a name, since she was the first to meet him," Craig concluded. "So do you have any ideas, honey?"

Delighted, Jody gazed at the dolphin on-screen. The underwater camera offered her a closer, clearer view than she'd had yet. For the first time, she noticed that the gray tones of his skin were not quite as uniform as they first appeared. There was a distinctive marking on the upper right side of his snout; an odd, curving shape that reminded her vaguely of an old-fashioned harp.

The harp made Jody think of music: of her recorder, which had first attracted the dolphin to the boat; and of the Ancient Greeks with their flutes. In the fifth grade, her class had done a unit on Greek mythology. She remembered the stories about the gods, and how each god had special characteristics. Suddenly, the perfect name slid into her mind . . .

"Apollo," she said.

"Apollo," Craig repeated, looking pleased. "The Greek god of music. That's right — aren't there stories that he took the form of a dolphin sometimes?"

Gina nodded. "Well done, Jody. It's a good name."

Dr. Jefferson Taylor said nothing.

4

"Excellent. I think we can send it to the TV station just as it is," Gina decided, after reviewing the underwater video footage she had taken of Apollo.

Dr. Taylor cleared his throat loudly. "Ahem . . . I think *I* should say something on the tape," he said.

Jody saw the surprise on her mother's face at this suggestion.

"Even *I'm* not doing an introduction," Gina explained. "The pictures speak for themselves. And the station manager at WDOL said they only want a minute or two of something light to tack onto the end of the news."

Dr. Taylor looked uncomfortable, then persisted. "I really do think I should mention that your video was made possible by my company's sponsorship," he said. "That's what I'm here for," he ended, looking a little embarrassed.

Jody saw her parents exchange a resigned glance, knowing that they couldn't really refuse.

"All right, I'll tape you," Gina agreed reluctantly. "But we'll have to keep it short. And the TV station may cut it anyway," she warned.

Dr. Taylor pretended not to hear this comment. "Now, where should I sit?" he asked, nervously straightening his collar and smoothing the little hair he had left. "Which do you think is my best angle?" he asked.

Jody couldn't stand to watch anymore. She had an idea. "Hey, Mom, is it all right if I use the new digital camera to take some pictures of Apollo? Then I can post them on the website."

Although she was looking strained from dealing with Dr. Taylor, Gina managed to smile at Jody. "Of course, sweetie," she replied. "You know how to use it."

"Just don't drop it in the water," Craig warned playfully, as Jody got the camera from its storage compartment.

"As if!" Jody answered.

She climbed up through the hatchway onto the deck, keeping a firm grip on the camera. She was careful where she put her feet, knowing how easy it would be to lose her balance on the unsteady surface of the rapidly moving boat. But though Jody was prepared for the changes underfoot as the boat lifted and fell against the waves, there was no way she could have been prepared for Brittany.

The other girl came charging across the deck, her face red with anger. Her seasickness had clearly disappeared. Jody saw that she was headed for the hatchway, and quickly moved to one side, out of her way.

As Brittany passed Jody, she gave her a deliberate, hard shove.

The push knocked Jody off balance. She would normally have kept on her feet by flinging out her arms, but she was clutching the camera tightly in both hands, and so she fell heavily onto her backside. "Ow!" she cried.

Cam hurried over to her. "Are you all right?" he asked, bending down to help her up, concern in his green eyes.

Jody took the hand he offered and got back onto her feet. "I'm okay, thanks," she said. She was more shocked than sore.

"That girl is a menace," said Cam angrily. "Yeah, I saw what she did." He shook his head. "Harry is trying his best. But she's impossible. If he tells her to do something, she'll go and do the opposite. I don't know how he keeps his temper."

Jody sighed, wondering how they were going to manage. "Somebody has to make her see that this boat is too small for her to go around acting like a three-year-old," she said.

"And soon!" Cam agreed, his voice grim.

"Is Apollo still around?" Jody asked, eager to change the subject.

"Who?" Cam looked puzzled.

"Oh, sorry," Jody smiled. "The dolphin — I've named him Apollo," she explained.

Cam shrugged. "Not sure," he said. "I've been busy with the equipment."

Jody went to the side of the deck and looked out over the sea. The wind whipped her hair about and chopped the water into hundreds of whitecaps. She saw several other yachts in the distance, nearer the shore. The brisk breeze made the sun's intense heat bearable; it was a glorious day for sailing. Behind her, she heard Cam commenting approvingly on their speed.

Where was Apollo? Had he felt abandoned when Gina left the water and they all went belowdecks? Jody wondered. Or had he lost interest when *Dolphin Dreamer* sailed on?

Her father came up beside her, muttering, "If I'd heard a lecture *that* dull in college, I would have dropped out. I hope Jefferson Taylor isn't going to insist on chipping in with his two cents' worth *every* time we send something to the media." He gave a gusty sigh. "Any sign of your friend?"

Jody shook her head, frowning with disappointment. "Do you think he's gone away for good? I wish now I'd stayed on deck and talked to him more."

She leaned out again, staring forward and narrowing her eyes against the bright sunshine. There! Was that him? Holding her breath, Jody saw the distinctive, finned shape of a dolphin, sleek and shining, as it glided through the water to one side and just ahead of the prow of *Dolphin Dreamer*, lifted and propelled by the wave that the yacht made in its progress.

She gasped with delight. "He's bow-riding," she cried.

"Which side?" Craig was immediately interested.

"Starboard!" Jody scrambled up to the forward deck for a closer view. Her father followed and they stood together gazing down at the dolphin. Jody could almost feel Apollo's pleasure in his "free ride" on the wave created by the boat. "It must be like surfing," she said. "Why do they do it?"

"Why do people surf?" Craig laughed. "Because it's fun."

Jody raised the camera. Just as she was framing a picture of the swimming dolphin, Apollo suddenly leaped clear of the wave he'd been riding. For one brilliant moment the dolphin's powerful, supple body hung in the air, and Jody pressed the shutter. She knew it would be a great picture. Then Apollo plunged back into the water.

Jody hastily pulled the camera close to her chest to

Apollo in action

keep it from getting splashed. "Thanks, Apollo," she called, laughing. "That was perfect!"

She took a few more pictures, and then gave the camera to her father to take down below.

"Don't you want to look at what you've taken?" he asked.

"Not yet. I'd rather watch the real thing!"

"A wise choice," Craig said with a grin. "I'm going to rescue your mother from Doctor Dull. I'm sure she'll want to come to see what Apollo is up to."

But when Gina came out on deck with her husband, Dr. Jefferson Taylor came, too.

"Mmm, a solitary bow-rider," he said. "I've read about that. But I had believed that was group behavior."

"Well, dolphins do usually travel in groups," Gina said. "We don't know whether this one is just temporarily separated from his group or if he's a loner."

"We might come across Apollo's school anytime now. Then we'd know," Jody suggested.

"Yes, we might," Craig said. "But it doesn't seem very likely now. Given the speed we're traveling, I'd expect to lose Apollo in the next couple of hours. The home range of the bottle-nosed in Florida is usually less than fifteen square miles."

"Don't they ever leave their home range?" Jody asked.

"Well, sure, for food if the fishing gets sparse," her father agreed. "And sometimes males will go in search of females, or migrate to another group with a different home range. And there might be other reasons why a dolphin would travel — we don't know as much about them as we'd like to think. But I've never heard of a dolphin leaving his home range to follow a boat. Not even a boat with someone as sweet as you on board."

Jody managed a weak smile in response. She reminded herself that Apollo was a wild creature, and only the first of many that she would meet. Yet she couldn't help feeling there was something special about him. She hated the thought of losing her new friend so soon.

"On the other hand," said Gina — as Dr. Taylor, looking thoughtful, left them and went back below — "some bottle-nosed dolphins have been tracked making regular journeys of more than one hundred eighty miles. We don't know where this one's come from, or where he might be going."

"I know where I'm going," said Craig. He patted his stomach. "Down below, to see if it's time for lunch yet."

"Coming, Jody?" her mother asked.

Jody looked out at Apollo, still enjoying his effortless ride on the bow wave. "I'll come down later," she said. "I just want to watch Apollo for a little longer."

As her parents left, she leaned against the rail on the prow and gazed down at the beautiful marine animal. Admiring the sleek lines of his body, she longed to sketch it, and wished she had a pad and pencil.

Hearing footsteps, Jody glanced around and was surprised to see Dr. Taylor heading her way. She looked away again, hoping he'd change his mind, but he came to stand immediately beside her and peered over the side.

"Still there," he muttered to himself. "Good. Now, just stay put, dolphin, so I can get you . . ." As he spoke he raised his hand, holding something that reflected the sunlight with a fierce, metallic glare.

Jody turned and stared. Her heart lurched in horror

as she saw not a camera in Dr. Taylor's hand, but a gun! And he was aiming it directly at Apollo.

"No!" she screamed and threw herself at him with all her might. He staggered, grunting, and rocked back on his heels, nearly losing his balance. He clutched desperately at the rigging with both hands to save himself. He had missed his shot, but he just managed to keep hold of the gun. Jody heard it clank against the stainless steel lines, and she was frightened. He might still use it on Apollo — or on her.

The sunglasses had slipped down Dr. Taylor's nose, and his watery brown eyes, angry and astonished, stared at Jody.

"I won't let you shoot him!" Jody cried passionately. "I won't let you hurt Apollo!"

"What on earth are you talking about? You crazy little girl —" he gasped breathlessly.

"What's the problem?" Craig came hurrying over to the forward deck, alerted by Jody's scream.

"Your daughter nearly pushed me overboard!" Dr. Taylor spluttered.

"He was going to shoot Apollo," Jody said, her eyes

appealing to her father for help. She saw his eyebrows go up as he noticed the gun.

"I had no idea anyone would be carrying a weapon on board, Dr. Taylor," Craig said grimly.

Squinting in the bright sunlight, Dr. Taylor straightened the sunglasses so they covered his eyes once more. He moved cautiously out of the rigging and displayed the gun, lying in the flat of his hand, to Jody's father. "This is not a weapon," he said stiffly. "Perhaps you don't recognize it, Dr. McGrath, because it is the very latest model. But if you examine it you will see that it is, in fact, a very sophisticated tagging device. And it cost a lot of money," he ended, glaring at Jody.

Craig took the instrument and whistled. "I've heard about these," he said.

Jody felt her own shoulders relax. She supposed she ought to apologize to Dr. Taylor, although she was still a little suspicious. "Sorry for pushing you over, Dr. Taylor," she said politely. "How does it work?"

Dr. Taylor grunted a grudging acceptance of Jody's apology, then explained how the tagging device worked. "It fires a dart, fitted with a microchip," he began. "Once embedded in the dolphin's flesh, the microchip provides information about the animal's movements."

"Embedded in the dolphin's flesh!" Jody repeated, dismayed. Perhaps she'd been right not to trust Dr. Taylor, after all. "Doesn't it hurt the dolphin?" she asked.

Dr. Taylor shrugged, as if he hadn't thought of this before. "I bought the equipment from a very reputable company . . ." he blustered.

"But dolphins have very sensitive skin, you know!" Jody insisted.

"Yes they do, honey," Craig agreed, putting a comforting arm around Jody's shoulder. "And some of the earlier methods of tagging probably did cause the dolphins some discomfort. In fact, some people still argue against any such tagging," he added, looking at Dr. Taylor.

The scientist's round face went even redder.

"But," Jody's father continued, "I think Dr. Taylor is right about this latest method — the darts are so tiny that the dolphin will feel only a tiny jab."

Jody trusted her father's judgment. But she didn't

think Dr. Taylor should be let off so lightly. "Would you let somebody shoot one of those things into *your* flesh?" she asked him.

"I wouldn't object," said Dr. Taylor loftily. "If it was in the interest of science, I would gladly agree to the slight discomfort."

Jody imagined a room full of scientists tracking Dr. Taylor's movements. She saw her father's mouth twitch and knew he was thinking the same thing.

"Well, now we've got that cleared up," Craig said, with a wink to Jody, "why don't we all go below for some lunch?"

"But what about my tagging?" said Dr. Taylor.

"Well, to be honest, I don't think it'll be much use here," Craig replied bluntly. "We'll soon sail out of the dolphin's range before you've had time to pick up any useful information on the tracking microchip."

Dr. Taylor sighed. "I hadn't thought of that," he said sorrowfully, as he followed everyone down to the galley.

Although Jody tried not to show it, she couldn't help

feeling cheered by the fact that Apollo had escaped being tagged.

"Never mind," said Gina to Dr. Taylor, as she was told about the recent drama on deck. "There'll be other chances. Here, have some of this chicken salad."

Dr. Taylor frowned, but accepted the plate she handed him. "Of course," he said. "And better ones. I'd rather track a dolphin that's part of a school, anyway."

After lunch, Jody settled down at her computer. Brittany had taken herself off, out of sight (and hearing!), to their cabin, and the twins were deeply absorbed — for once — in some computer game on their own computer at the other end of the main cabin.

Jody enjoyed the peace and quiet, looking at her pictures of Apollo and choosing the best one to post on the website. She also wrote a description of what she'd seen, and then wrote a long e-mail to Lindsay. She filled in her best friend on everything that had been happening, especially enjoying the chance to let off steam about Brittany and to describe her first encounter with a wild dolphin. Jody wished Lindsay could have been with her, and for the first time she realized just how much she was going to miss her friend.

That afternoon passed swiftly and peacefully. Then, toward evening, the motion of the boat changed dramatically. The smooth sailing had ended; it felt as if they were being dragged roughly over a very rocky road.

Jody couldn't concentrate with all the jouncing and bouncing. She was logging off her computer as Brittany came reeling out of their cabin, groaning loudly. She looked positively green.

"I'm going to be sick!" she cried loudly.

Maddie had been working across the table from Jody. She jumped up as soon as Brittany appeared and spoke sympathetically but firmly. "Get up on deck. I'll come with you. In fact, let's all go. We'll all feel better and we could ask Harry if it's possible to change course to find a gentler motion."

But when they emerged on deck, it seemed a different world from the clear and brilliant day Jody remembered from earlier. Dark clouds lowered overhead and lightning flared against the sky behind them.

Harry was far too absorbed in the demands of steering the boat through such a rough sea to pay much attention to the woes of a seasick crew.

When Maddie asked if he could change course, he shook his head grimly, and spoke above the noise of the rising wind and sea. "I've just changed course," he said. "We need more speed, not less!" He broke off to shout orders to Cam and Craig. Then, turning back, he added, "I'm sorry you're finding it a bit rough, but it would be worse if we took a different direction." He took a deep breath and gazed ahead. "There's a big storm on the way," he explained, "and we've got to try to outrun it."

5

Jody was immediately caught up in the excitement of the attempt to outrun the storm. The sails billowed, then swelled tautly as they came into the wind. *Dolphin Dreamer* surged forward, almost flying, as light and fast as a dream.

Brittany, beside her at the rail, already looked better, her seasickness helped by the smoother motion of the boat and the fresh air on her face. Jody was glad for her. She'd been seasick herself a few times, and it really was no fun.

Jody gazed out to sea, wondering where Apollo was, and if dolphins were even aware of storms. Probably the weather on the surface wouldn't make much difference to their lives.

She gasped as she was suddenly drenched with water. But it was fresh, not seawater. It was rain. Fast as the *Dolphin Dreamer* had flown, the rain clouds had been faster.

"Prepare to come about!" shouted the captain, giving the command to change course. Cam, Gina, and Craig scrambled to obey, slackening the sails. They hadn't managed to outrun the rain. Now the squall was so fierce that they could hardly see any distance ahead. It wasn't safe to keep going.

"You girls get below!" Maddie shouted as she rushed forward to help Cam reef the foresail. Taking it down would reduce their speed.

Jody's heart lurched and she clutched the rail to save herself as the deck pitched sharply beneath her feet.

Brittany cried out in fright. "What's happening?"

"We're going to heave to," Jody said. "That means

we're stopping — as much as we can. We'll drift a little, but we have to batten down and ride it out."

"Passengers below!" bellowed Harry from the helm. "Now!"

"He means us," said Jody urgently, putting one hand on Brittany's shoulder. "Come on. We're in the way."

"No! I'm not going!" Brittany shouted, setting her jaw stubbornly.

Cam was right, thought Jody. Brittany just wouldn't do anything her father said. She decided to try another angle. "You can't want to stay out in this awful rain! Come below where it's dry."

Brittany already looked as if she couldn't get any wetter. She shook her head stubbornly. "I feel sick when I'm inside. I'm staying right here." She straightened up, as if to emphasize her words, and moved toward the center of the boat.

It was the wrong move. Jody — an experienced sailor — had seen that Cam was releasing the boom, the long horizontal pole that supported the mainsail and enabled them to change direction. She heard his shouted warning — which Brittany was too absorbed by her own problems to notice. The heavy boom was swinging in their direction, straight for Brittany's head.

There was no time to explain. Jody grabbed the other girl by the arm and yanked her to one side. A split second later the boom swung by, narrowly missing them.

Brittany stared at Jody through narrowed eyes, then lashed out at her, reacting as if Jody was attacking her instead of trying to save her.

Jody tried to dodge Brittany's blow, but just then the boat heeled over sharply, pitching her forward. She flailed around for something to grab hold of, but there was only Brittany. And as Jody grabbed her again, Brittany's face blazed red. She shoved Jody away as hard as she could. Jody staggered backward and, with a feeling of complete disbelief, she felt herself go flying overboard.

It happened in an instant, yet on her way into the heaving sea below, time seemed to stretch out. Jody had time to feel shocked that it was really happening to her, to feel angry at Brittany, and annoyed at herself for being so careless! She also managed to hold her breath before she plunged below the water.

Quickly, Jody struggled back to the surface, pulse racing, adrenaline coursing through her system. She was a strong, experienced swimmer, and — like the rest of her family — Jody had practiced what to do if this ever happened.

Of course, in the practice sessions the sea had never been as rough as this, and it hadn't been raining so hard she could scarcely see.

But, as scared as Jody felt, at least she wasn't injured . . . and surely Brittany would have alerted everyone to what had happened. Her parents and the rest of the crew would already be looking for her. They'd locate her very soon, then Cam would attach the ladder, and she'd be back on board. All she had to do was keep herself afloat and stay near to the boat.

But where *was* the boat? She should have been right next to it, but she couldn't see it. All of a sudden Jody was completely terrified. She was lost!

Gasping for breath, her heart pounding, Jody strug-

Overboard!

gled to stay calm, remembering how her dad had emphasized the importance of keeping a clear head in a crisis. The boat *couldn't* have disappeared. She must have gotten turned around while she was underwater, that was all.

Blinking hard against the blinding rain, and trying to keep on top of the waves that threatened to submerge her, Jody paddled around in a circle, searching desperately in the featureless gray water for the shape that meant safety.

There it was! But it was so far away! Jody felt a sinking feeling in her stomach. She knew that she couldn't stay where she was and wait to be found. Her family would never see her from that distance.

Grimly determined, trying not to think about the difficulty of it, Jody began swimming toward *Dolphin Dreamer*.

Swimming was hard work in the rain and wind, and the waves all seemed determined to push her back. Jody managed to kick her shoes off. They were still-new sneakers that she hated to lose, but in the water they were heavy, making it harder to swim. Feet bare, she took a deep breath and plunged on. She kept her head down and swam steadily and fast as if in a grim race. But every time she stopped to get her bearings, *Dolphin Dreamer* seemed as far away as ever. What was going on?

Jody's heart sank as she finally realized the boat had still been moving when she fell overboard, and even with the sails all stowed, it was still likely to drift. As fast as she was swimming toward it, the wind and currents were taking it farther away. It must be moving much faster than she was. She was never going to catch up to it.

Jody nearly burst into tears of terror. But she didn't have the energy to spare. She *couldn't* give up now, she just couldn't. She had to hope that Brittany really had raised the alarm, and that her family would be looking for her — though she couldn't see any sign of that from the boat. By now, people should have been hanging over the sides, looking for her, calling her name.

Jody tried calling to them. "Help! Help!" Her voice sounded terrifyingly small in the vast waters, and when she opened her mouth to call a third "Help!" a wave splashed against her face. She gagged and choked on the salt.

The rain was still coming down in sheets, making it hard to breathe or to see. She prayed that the boat might be moving toward her instead of away. They *must* be looking for her, they must! Maybe she hadn't really been in the water as long as it seemed.

Gasping, panting, desperate, Jody forced herself to keep swimming toward *Dolphin Dreamer.* No matter how hard it was, she would just have to keep going. She would get there eventually. She was exhausted, but she wouldn't give in.

Then Jody saw something which turned her blood to ice. A dark, curving fin cut through the waves . . . vanished . . . then appeared again a few yards away. *Shark.*

She tried desperately to think of what to do, but the only advice she could remember — get out of the water — was utterly useless to her now. Sharks were deadly, but unpredictable. If this one wasn't hungry, it might simply swim past her. But if it *was* hungry, she wouldn't stand a chance.

The fin vanished . . . then appeared again, closer. Jody clutched the silver dolphin on her necklace tightly between thumb and forefinger. If she had ever needed luck in her life, it was now. The fin vanished.

Beneath the water, Jody felt something bump against her legs. She gave a yelp. She couldn't help herself. But then, as she felt the gentle pressure against her legs, she realized that what she was feeling wasn't the rough hide of a shark, but the smooth skin of a dolphin. "*Apollo?*" she breathed.

The distinctive head of a bottle-nosed dolphin broke through the surface. It *was* Apollo! Jody was immediately awed by just how big the dolphin was, close-up. Her mother had estimated Apollo's length as almost three yards. But it was one thing to watch at a distance while her mother swam with Apollo, and quite another to be in the water herself with such a large animal.

Jody wasn't scared, though. How could she be? This was Apollo. She looked him right in the eye. It was large, round, brown, and shining with unmistakable intelligence. There was something about the dolphin that made Jody feel peaceful. For a moment she almost forgot the danger she was in.

Apollo nudged her hand. Jody was amazed. He had avoided her mother's touch, yet he was inviting *her* to touch him. He moved to bring the dorsal fin on his back under her fingers.

Jody suddenly guessed what was being offered. "You'll tow me back to the boat?" Scarcely daring to believe it, she flung her arm around the dolphin's smooth, streamlined back, hooking her hand around the dorsal fin as a means of hanging on.

As soon as Jody was in place, Apollo began swimming — a gentle, powerful motion that pulled her rapidly through the water.

Although Jody realized Apollo was moving slowly by dolphin standards — probably out of concern for her — the sensation of being pulled through the waves by such a gentle, yet powerful, force was exhilarating. Jody began to grin. After the terror of the last few minutes, the delight she felt now was making her giddy. She knew she was safe, now, with Apollo.

Blinking against the slackening rain, Jody saw *Dolphin Dreamer*, seeming to grow larger by the second as she drew closer. Everyone was on deck, leaning over the sides, most of them in brilliantly colored rain gear.

They were all looking for her. When she was close enough to see her mother's desperately worried face, Jody cried out, "Ahoy!"

As Gina saw her daughter her expression changed to amazement, then lit up with an almost disbelieving joy.

Apollo took Jody to the side of the boat where the ladder had been hung out.

"Thanks, Apollo," Jody said, feeling her heart thud with relief. She seized hold of the ladder and began to climb up. Suddenly, it was all too much. She came to the end of her strength. Her legs started trembling and one foot slipped on the step, but before she could fall, her father's strong arms grasped her and he lifted her up and into the boat as if she weighed no more than a baby.

"Thank goodness," he murmured, holding her close. "Thank goodness you're safe."

Explanations waited — by Craig's order — until Jody was washed and dried, snugly dressed in a comfortable sweatsuit, and curled up on a seat in the main cabin with a steaming mug of soup provided by Mei Lin. Everyone except Cam, who was taking the watch on deck, gathered around.

Jody felt a little flustered at being the center of attention. Everyone was staring at her as if she'd performed a miracle, when really it was Apollo who deserved all the credit.

"I can't believe we almost lost you!" Gina said. She clutched her daughter's free hand as if she would never let it go again. "Thank goodness Brittany saw you go overboard and raised the alarm. What if no one had seen?"

Craig nodded. "That could easily have happened. Things here were pretty chaotic around then. The Genoa ripped while we were reefing it, and then — as if a ripped sail wasn't bad enough — one of the shrouds snapped! I thought we were going to lose the mast. Believe me, nobody had time to notice who was there and who wasn't," he ended seriously.

Gina shuddered, then flashed a warm smile of thanks at Brittany. But the girl was staring down at her feet and did not respond. Gina turned to Jody. "So what happened?" she demanded, squeezing Jody's hand. "I thought you kids had all been told to get below. How did you happen to be on deck, never mind go overboard?"

As Jody hesitated, Brittany suddenly came to life. Throwing her head back she declared, "It was an accident! Jody pushed me — to get me out of the way, so I wouldn't get hit in the head — but I —"

Jody leaped in. "Yeah, that's right! We were just about to go below when I noticed the boom heading for us, so I pushed Brittany out of the way — and then I was trying to duck the boom myself, so I wasn't paying attention when the boat suddenly heeled — and whoosh, I went right over the side! It was a complete accident." She stopped, breathless.

Brittany stared at Jody, shocked, her mouth still open. And then, as she realized that Jody had saved her again, the color began to creep back into her pale cheeks. "Yeah, thanks, Jody," she murmured quietly.

It seemed that Brittany was thanking Jody for saving her from being hit on the head by the boom. But Jody knew that Brittany was also thanking her for keeping her out of a great deal of trouble. "You're welcome," Jody replied. But she gave the other girl a meaningful look, and hoped Brittany would understand it: ***I didn't rat on you, but you'll have to shape up.***

"Now tell us about the dolphin, Jody!" urged Sean.

"Yeah!" said Jimmy. "Tell us how he towed you! Did you really think he was a shark?"

6

When they were alone in their cabin that night, Brittany spoke in a voice Jody hadn't heard her use before — ashamed and nervous. "Thanks again for not telling on me."

"There wasn't any reason to. I'm not mad at you." Jody spoke honestly. In fact, now that the shock had passed, all she could think of was how wonderful Apollo had been. She almost felt grateful to the other girl, but she certainly wasn't going to tell her that, in case she got the wrong idea!

Brittany stared, wide-eyed. "But I could have *killed* you!"

"But you didn't," Jody pointed out. Then, curious, she asked, "What *did* you intend to do?"

Brittany collapsed onto her bunk and gazed pleadingly at Jody. "I just got mad. I just wanted to teach you a lesson, not . . ." Her voice trailed off and her face went pale as she thought again about what might have happened. "I didn't think. I was scared when I saw you fall over the side! I could hardly believe it."

Jody decided to take advantage of Brittany's guilty feelings. "Look, Brittany, things are different at sea. You may not like it, but everybody on board has to obey the captain. You have to do what Harry says — not because he's your dad, but because he's in charge of the boat. He has to make the decisions about our safety. If the crew starts arguing with him, or takes their time about following orders, it could be a disaster. Do you understand?"

A stubborn expression flashed across Brittany's mouth, but then she nodded. "I guess . . . while we're on board." Then, all in a rush, she said, "And I promise I won't push you or hit you again. It was a babyish thing to do, and I never thought it could be so dangerous!" She took a deep breath. "I'm sorry."

It was clear that apologizing did not come easily to Brittany Pierce.

The morning dawned bright and still. The fierce squalls of the night before weren't even a memory in the achingly clear blue sky. The adults discussed their options and decided that, rather than motoring in to the nearest port, they would stay put and make their own repairs to the boat. This was unlikely to take more than two days. If they found they needed any replacement parts, they'd head for Key West.

Jody was glad. Now she knew they were still in Apollo's home territory, and she could look forward to spending more time with her new friend. Although she couldn't spot him in the water around the boat when she looked before breakfast, she had a feeling that he wasn't far away. Surely he would turn up before long.

"May I go swimming this morning?" Jody asked her mother over breakfast.

Gina smiled. "You mean you didn't get enough of being in the sea yesterday?"

"Nope. Do you think that means I'm half dolphin?" Jody teased.

"I think it means you're half mad, like the rest of this crazy family." Gina laughed and leaned over to hug her daughter.

"So is that a yes?" Jody pressed her mother eagerly.

"Sure, why not?" Gina looked across the table at the twins, who were as alert as puppies at the mention of a walk. "I think we all might enjoy a swim this morning, before it gets too hot."

Sean and Jimmy whistled and cheered their approval.

Even Brittany looked a little brighter at the idea of a swim, although she turned to Maddie to ask, "Is it really safe to swim out there?"

"If you're not a confident swimmer, you should wear a life vest," Maddie suggested.

"I'm an excellent swimmer," Brittany protested. "We have a pool at home, and I swim every day."

"Well, then, you'll be fine here. The sea looks practically as still as a swimming pool this morning." Maddie smiled warmly and laid her knife and fork on her empty plate.

"But what about . . . sharks and things like that?" Brittany asked, lowering her voice a little.

"We won't go in if there's any sign of sharks," Maddie assured her. "And we can ask Cam to keep a shark-watch from the deck."

"Race you!" said Jimmy to Sean.

Gina held up a warning hand. "We'll meet on deck in our swimming things in one hour, not before." She pressed on over the noisy groans of the twins. "Nobody is going in the water before their breakfast has had time to digest. We don't want anybody getting cramps."

Jody spent the time updating her diary about the exciting events of the day before. Then she quickly changed into her swimsuit and went up on deck.

As she emerged from the hold, Jody heard something that made her heart beat faster. First there was a whistle; then a series of rapid, stuttering clicks and pops — the unmistakable sounds of a dolphin. "Apollo!" she cried joyfully, rushing to the side where her parents were standing.

At the sight of her, Apollo whistled again and leaped into the air. As the spray rained down on her, Jody laughed with delight. "How long has he been here?"

"Less than a minute, honestly," her mother replied. "I was just going to call you."

"Can I go in with him? Please?" Jody looked hopefully at her mother.

At that moment, Sean and Jimmy erupted out of the hold, wearing matching fluorescent orange swimming trunks and goggles, yelling with excitement, their bare feet slapping the deck. They launched themselves off the side, knees up — to splash bottoms down like a couple of human cannonballs.

Gina winced and sighed. "Of course you can."

Craig had peeled off his T-shirt. "I'd better go and keep an eye on those two."

Watch out dolphins — here comes trouble!

"I'll join you in a minute," Gina agreed. She turned to look at the hatchway. "Oh, good, here come Brittany and Maddie."

Jody was too excited about another chance to swim with Apollo to wait another minute. She fitted on her goggles. Then, taking a deep breath, she dived off the side of the boat.

After the heat of the sun, the water was cool and welcoming as Jody sliced cleanly into it. It was a different world down here, the world the dolphins knew as home. Underwater, the sounds of her brothers' yells were muffled. She saw their pale legs kicking and waving in the dim, greenish water, like the tentacles of some strange creature. She turned her head, and there, only a few inches away, was Apollo. He gazed at her sidelong, out of one eye.

Jody ran out of breath and had to shoot back to the surface to breathe again. Apollo poked his beak out of the water, continuing to watch her. This time there was no pounding rain to blur her vision. She saw him more clearly than ever before. For the first time she noticed the little dimples on his head that marked where his ears would be.

"Hi there," she said quietly. "I'm really glad you came back."

She reached out to stroke him, and he let her. His skin felt smooth and finely ridged beneath her fingertips. She was careful to avoid the blowhole on the top of his head.

He dipped below the water and rolled onto his back, letting her stroke his paler belly, almost as if he were a cat or a dog.

"Hey, that's just like Fluffy used to do," said Jimmy.

Jody was startled. She had been so absorbed in Apollo that she hadn't noticed her brothers approach. Apollo rolled again and disappeared beneath the surface.

Taking a deep breath, Jody sank down and went after him. But speed was so natural to the dolphin that he shot away out of sight in an instant. Jody flailed around for a few more seconds, trying to see where he'd gone, then gave up and surfaced again.

"Where'd he go?" asked Sean.

Before she could reply, up popped Apollo.

"I want to touch him," Jimmy said, and began to swim toward the dolphin. Although the twins normally did things together, Sean hung back, saying nothing, looking thoughtful.

But Apollo wouldn't let Jimmy near enough to be touched. He shot away with a simple, effortless flex of his body.

"How can he go so fast?" Sean asked.

"Their bodies are perfectly designed for speed — streamlined and very powerful," answered his father. "There's no boat that can match them — and, believe me, boat designers have tried to learn from dolphins! One of the reasons they can go so fast is that the dolphin's body constantly changes shape while swimming. And their skin secretes an oil that helps reduce friction, helping them to glide through the water."

"That must be why his skin feels so smooth," said Jody.

Jimmy pouted. "I want to feel it. Make him let me," he begged Jody.

"He's not my pet, Jimmy. I can't *make* him do anything," Jody said reasonably.

"He gave you a ride yesterday," Jimmy pointed out.

Jody shrugged. "That was his decision," she replied, and began to swim away from her brother.

Jimmy scowled. "Aw, I want him to give me a tow! How'd you get him to?" A cunning look crept across his face. "I know! Like this!" He began to flail and splash and sputter. "Help! Help! I'm drowning! Help me, Apollo!"

"Knock it off, Jimmy," Craig said sharply. "Any more of that, and you're back on the boat."

Jimmy's clumsy acting did not fool Apollo. Gazing around at the remarkably still water, Jody caught sight of the dolphin swimming beneath the surface, not far away. He must have been aware of Jimmy's antics, but had decided to ignore them. She filled her lungs with air and dived down.

Apollo swam to meet her and they gazed at each other for a long moment underwater. Then he moved closer and nudged her hand. She stroked his nose. He made a soft clicking noise and opened his mouth. Jody stared at the small, sharply pointed teeth that lined his jaw, before he clacked it shut again. His clicks became more rapid. She had the sense that he was trying to say something to her, but what was it? Would she ever understand? A desperate need for air forced her to return to the surface.

As Jody came up, she saw that her mother had also entered the water, although there was no sign of Brittany or Maddie. This seemed odd, but Jody had no time to think about it, because just then she felt something nudge the back of her knees.

It was Apollo, of course. What was he doing? Jody gasped, astonished, as she felt herself being pushed and lifted from below. Her legs slipped over either side of the dolphin's sleek hide; her arms flailed for balance. She found herself sitting on the dolphin's back. She was riding Apollo!

It was like a dream, like the best dream Jody had ever had. She sat straight and tall and fearless, gripping the animal with her knees, letting herself be carried. It was absolutely magical!

Jody saw the amazement on her parents' faces as

they treaded water and gazed at her. She heard the shouts of the twins and Maddie was calling something from the deck of the boat. But they all seemed very far away, in another world entirely, as she was carried smoothly and swiftly over the water, in a big, arcing circle around *Dolphin Dreamer*.

It ended some timeless minutes later, with Apollo dropping a little lower in the water. Jody knew somehow what he meant and loosened the grip of her legs, slipping down and then letting him swim away.

She swam idly — still half in a dream, still feeling the wonderful sensation of being carried along by the fast, powerful animal who had chosen her for his friend. She felt blessed, enchanted. She drifted onto her back and floated there, gazing up into the blue, blue sky.

7

June 22 — 11:50 p.m.

This has been the most wonderful day of my life.

Brittany's asleep. I can hear her snoring in the bunk below. I should really be sleeping, too, but I'm still excited — I got to ride Apollo! I can't stop thinking about it and wondering what it meant.

Dr. Taylor thinks that Apollo must have been a performing dolphin who was taught that riding trick before being released into the wild. But I don't think that's true. I'm sure he's a wild dolphin. If he'd been trained to come to people, why didn't he let Jimmy or Mom touch him? Why only me?

Dad says there are stories going back to ancient times about special friendships between dolphins and humans. Young boys used to ride on the backs of dolphins in the Mediterranean. I remember reading about a girl in New Zealand who swam every day with a friendly wild dolphin who eventually let her ride him.

Brittany never did come swimming with us. I don't know why. She got very huffy when I asked. She said she preferred to talk to Maddie, who's "really cool." I guess it's good that there is at least someone on board who Brittany will listen to, but even when Maddie dived into the water, Brittany stayed on deck.

I wonder if Brittany could be scared of dolphins? But that's just crazy. Maybe she has confused them with sharks — after all, she did think they were fish. I tried to find out, but she just got nasty. She's keeping her promise not to push or hit (so far!) but she still doesn't like me, and she sure lets me know it.

In the morning, while Brittany was still sleeping, Jody dressed hastily in a clean T-shirt and shorts, grabbed her recorder, and left. There was a smell of fresh coffee wafting from the galley, but no sign or sound of anyone else until she reached the deck, where she found her father.

"Hi, what are you doing up?" he asked in surprise.

"Same as you?" Jody lifted her face to the sun and sniffed the fresh, salty air.

He shook his head. "It's my watch. Everybody else is still asleep. It's still very early, you know."

"Oh. Well, would it disturb anybody if I practiced my recorder?" she asked.

Craig smiled. "A little dawn music would be lovely. Think you could whistle up a wind?"

Jody cocked her head, looking puzzled.

"It's a sailor's superstition. When it's calm, you're supposed to be able to raise a wind by whistling," her father explained.

"I won't whistle, then," she said fervently. "I hope it stays dead calm for days and days and we can just stay here and do some scuba diving. I haven't had a chance to dive yet, remember."

"Do you think Apollo would have given you a ride

yesterday if you'd had your scuba gear on?" Her father gave her a teasing grin.

Jody laughed. "No, probably not! But if you really want to know about dolphins you have to get right down under the water with them — to see life the way they see it, don't you?"

"Hmm, I couldn't have put it better myself," said Craig, his blue-gray eyes sparkling with mischief. "In fact, I think I may have put it exactly like that at some point. What a lucky man I am, to have a daughter who listens to me!"

Jody wrinkled her nose. "Well, now you can listen to me for a change." She waved her recorder like a wand at her father, then went up to the forward deck.

She'd intended to sit exactly where she'd been the first time Apollo had responded to her playing, but what she found lying there made her stop and stare down at her feet in surprise. It was a small blue-gray fish about twenty inches in length; nothing extraordinary about it except for the magnificent, iridescent wings attached to its sides — a flying fish!

Jody tucked her recorder under one arm and picked up the fish. She felt it quiver in her hands. It was still alive! Quickly, she tossed it over the side, then ran back to tell her father.

Craig nodded, unsurprised. "I've thrown back half a dozen this morning. Later on we might want to keep them to eat."

"Do they taste good?" Jody grimaced, not sure she would want to eat something that looked like that.

Her father grinned at her. "Depends on how hungry you are."

"They don't really fly, do they?" Jody was curious.

"No, but they can glide — up to about a hundred yards. Their wings are really fins, which they keep tucked against their sides while they're swimming. If they're chased by another fish, or sense danger, they launch themselves upward, taxi across the surface of the water, and then take off and glide to safety." Craig stuck his arms straight out to show what he meant.

Jody stared at the sea, shining in the early sun. "Could they have been chased by dolphins?"

"I guess so. But I haven't seen any," he said. Jody's

shoulders drooped. Craig patted her back. "Go on, go play your flute."

"It's a recorder, Dad," Jody corrected him.

"Whatever." Craig shrugged his shoulders, then gave Jody a little wave as she left him to return to the foredeck.

She played the few pieces she knew by heart, gazing out to sea all the while. But no matter how hard she looked, there was no sight of a dark fin in the distance, and no head poked up out of the water to whistle back at her. An idea slipped into her mind, making her unhappy. What if she never saw Apollo again, and he had known all along? What if that fantastic ride had been his way of saying a special good-bye?

There would be other dolphins, she knew, but she couldn't believe she would ever meet another one who would be as special to her as Apollo.

By the time she gave up her solo concert — bored with repeating the same few pieces — a breeze had picked up, ruffling her hair and clanging the halyards against the mast.

When Jody joined the others belowdecks at the

breakfast table, she wasn't surprised to hear Harry Pierce proposing that they should set sail again, to take advantage of the wind, as soon as possible. The necessary repairs had been made, and there was no point in just sitting around, especially if there were no dolphins to study.

The prospect of moving on seemed to cheer everyone else. But Gina must have sensed Jody's unspoken sadness, for she touched her hair and murmured, "If it's not too rough this afternoon we'll do some diving — how's that?"

"That would be great," Jody said, and meant it. Even if Apollo wasn't around, scuba was one of the coolest things she knew how to do. Almost as good as riding a dolphin!

The morning passed slowly. Mei Lin was baking bread. Jody had wanted to help, but Brittany had got in first, and there wasn't room in the tiny galley for more than two people. It was her brothers' turn for a sailing lesson from Harry. Jody was feeling left out and bored when the shout came from her father on deck, "Dolphins off the port bow!"

Jody bolted for the hatchway.

On deck, she hurried to join her father at the rail, where he was gazing out to sea, along with her mother and the twins. What she saw took her breath away.

It was a whole school of dolphins, moving so rapidly that it was impossible to say how many there were. Thirty? Fifty? More? Dark fins dotted the waves, and sleek, leaping gray bodies leaped here and there, back and forth. It was an amazing sight!

The twins were shouting with excitement. Jody made room for Maddie and Cam, who'd also come rushing over. Even Dr. Taylor had come up on deck to see what all the fuss was about.

Harry Pierce, at the helm, gave a roar of laughter. "Honestly, if I didn't know better, I'd say you were a bunch of tourists!"

Through her excitement, Jody felt guilty, and she saw from the rueful look her parents exchanged that they felt the same.

Jimmy said, "We're going up front, okay?"

"Forward," said Sean. "The word is forward."

"Go ahead," said Craig. "But be careful. I'm not sure

I'll be able to convince Harry to go back for you if you fall in."

"I'm going down for my camera," said Gina. "This is just too gorgeous."

Jody stared in wonder as three dolphins all leaped out of the water in different parts of the group, slapping the water with their tails, then diving down again.

"What are they *doing*?" Only when Brittany spoke did Jody realize the other girl had also come on deck, and was now standing between her and Dr. Taylor.

"They're feeding," Craig replied. "At this distance it is hard to be certain, but I would guess that they've trapped a school of fish. They do that by forcing the fish upward against the surface of the water. Some of the dolphins will be swimming back and forth underneath, to keep the fish trapped, while others take turns snatching a mouthful. Still other dolphins will chase back any of the fish that manage to break away."

Gina returned with her camera and began filming. Under the captain's skillful control, they were sailing nearer to the dolphin group.

Lunchtime for dolphins

"Why do they jump up and slap their tails?" Brittany asked. "That wouldn't stop the fish from getting away."

Jody was curious about this, too. Perhaps it's joyful behavior, she thought, a way of expressing excitement at finding so much food.

Her mother gave them a more scientific explanation: "Slapping the water makes a loud, sharp sound," she said. "Loud noises frighten the fish, making them gather together into a tighter ball, instead of trying to get away."

"So dolphins aren't just these totally sweet and friendly little angels," said Brittany.

"Of course not," objected Dr. Taylor, sounding shocked. "Dolphins are predators. They are hunters."

Jody knew Brittany's comment was aimed at her. "They have to catch the fish to live," she said defensively. "They have to eat, just like we do. But they only kill fish and squid and things like that," she added, eager to impress upon the other girl that dolphins weren't to be feared.

Jody had noticed two or three seagulls hovering

over the feeding dolphins. More appeared, out of the blue, until there was a screaming mob of birds darting toward the water, then flapping up again, sometimes with fish in their beaks.

"Hey, look, the birds are stealing the dolphins' lunch!" Cam laughed.

"Not exactly," said Craig. "Some of the fish try to escape by leaping into the air — those are the ones the birds pick off. Plenty for all. You'll often find seabirds following a school of dolphins, just waiting for a chance like this."

After a few more minutes, the birds flew away and the dolphins began to leave. Feeding time was over. Jody and the others watched as the sleek, leaping gray-finned bodies swam farther out to sea and were gradually lost to sight.

Jody sighed. She had been holding her breath, hoping the dolphins would come their way. She wondered if Apollo had been part of that big group. She knew that one of the reasons dolphins traveled in herds was that it made hunting easier. They could get more fish by working together than they could alone. It would be a hard life for Apollo if he was on his own.

For lunch there was fresh warm bread, cheese, and gazpacho — a cold vegetable soup.

Between hungry bites, Jody paused briefly to ask, "Mei, did you ever see dolphins when you were in China?"

Mei Lin nodded. "Once, only. But it was not like your dolphins. I was lucky enough to see a baiji."

"What's a baiji?" Sean demanded.

"It's the rarest dolphin in the world," Craig explained for the benefit of all. "It's found only in parts of one river in China."

"Really, Mei Lin?" said Gina in surprise. "You actually saw a baiji?"

"Yes, I think so. I was only a little girl at the time, and it was early in the morning and very misty. I was traveling with my parents in a boat on the Yangtze River. I heard a sound like a sneeze from the water, and I looked over the side and saw a smooth, grayish animal with a long, skinny nose swimming away. My father said this was one of China's national treasures. But later I was told by someone else that it could not have been the baiji that I saw. It must have been only a porpoise, because the baiji are too shy to let themselves be seen. I don't know. My father was not an expert. But I like to think we saw a baiji."

"You were very lucky if you did," said her mother. "It's been a protected species since 1975, but there are probably less than fifty left today. The Yangtze is one of the busiest waterways in the world, and as the baiji won't live anywhere else, there's not a lot that can be done to save them."

Gina's words made Jody feel gloomy. She knew that all over the world cetaceans — both dolphins and whales — were at risk, but usually there was something that could be done to help the various species to survive. Commercial whaling could be stopped, destructive fishing methods changed, pollution controlled. People's efforts could make a major difference. The oceans were vast, and most dolphin species numbered in the thousands. But for an animal whose habitat was restricted to a part of one river, the future did not look bright. Even declaring it a protected species was probably not enough.

There was only one thing that could have cheered Jody's gloomy thoughts — and it actually happened.

"Dolphins approaching! Port *and* starboard sides!" Harry's voice came bellowing down from the deck, like a foghorn.

The McGraths and Maddie abandoned their food and made a dash for the deck, Jody ahead of them all. At the front of her mind was one thought: Apollo! Has he come back?

8

There were six bottle-nosed dolphins swimming around the boat, poking their heads curiously out of the water and jostling for position, as if for a better view. One would suddenly dive down and disappear for a moment, only to appear a moment later on the other side of the boat. They also nudged the boat with their beaks, and one rubbed sidelong against it as if he had an itch.

"Do you see your friend out there?" Craig asked Jody.

Was Apollo one of the six? Jody frowned uncertainly,

and leaned out over the side, trying to get a better view.

The dolphins didn't make it easy for her. They were in constant motion, diving and resurfacing, swimming back and forth, slipping in and out of sight. They were all practically identical — at least, from her position on deck she couldn't tell them apart. Maybe if she was closer she would be able to see that one carried that funny, curving little mark on the side of Apollo's beak. But if he *was* one of the group, Jody felt sure he would draw attention to himself in some way, maybe give her a special greeting.

These dolphins, although they were vocalizing, clicking and whistling and blowing, seemed to be talking to one another, not to her. She shook her head regretfully in answer to her father's question. "No, I don't think so."

"They're all very similar to Apollo," said Craig. "They seem to be roughly the same age, the sort of group I would expect to find him spending most of his time with after leaving his mother."

"What age would that be?" she asked.

"For the bottle-nosed, it's about four years," her father replied. "The younger ones travel with their mothers' group."

"Do you think these are all boys?" Jody asked curiously.

Her father shook his head. "Probably not, if this is a group of sub-adults, as I think. They're the dolphin equivalent of human teenagers — a gang of friends hanging out together, boys and girls. Older adult males tend to travel in smaller groups, and adult females usually rejoin their mother's group. But sometimes adult males will be found with groups of mothers and calves. It's almost as hard to predict a bottle-nosed group as it is to describe the 'typical' human family!" He grinned.

"And of course, they'll gather together in the hundreds sometimes, to cooperate in a hunt, or if danger threatens," Gina put in. "People do that, too. If we weren't part of human society wouldn't it seem just as difficult to explain?" She lowered the hydrophone over the side of the boat into the water, to record the sounds the dolphins made.

Jody loved listening to the clicks, pops, creaks, and

whistles that seemed so full of meaning. She firmly believed dolphins had their own language, and she had a dream that someday she would be able to understand it. She knew that researchers had been working on the puzzle for ages, and that most had decided that dolphin sounds were more like birdsong than any human language. But history was full of experts who had been proved wrong. Maybe when she grew up she would design a computer program that could translate "Dolphinese" into English!

Dr. Jefferson Taylor hauled himself out of the hatchway onto the deck. He was not wearing his sunglasses, but had put on a wide-brimmed straw hat. He was carrying a small canvas bag. He paused, removed a handkerchief from his pocket, and mopped his face, sighing, "I'd really like to rest for a little while after that delicious meal," he said. "But I'm afraid I'm someone who just can't rest if there's work to be done!"

He strolled over to the side. "Ah, a nice-sized subgroup this time," he said with satisfaction. "Dr. McGrath, I trust there won't be any objection if I tag one of these specimens?"

Jody tensed anxiously. She felt like shouting at him that they weren't specimens, they were dolphins, but she felt her father's hand rest warningly on her back and she kept quiet.

She saw her parents exchange a glance. Gina said, "Of course, that's fine. But as Craig mentioned to you before, we are on the move and we can't guarantee to stay within the dolphin's range."

Dr. Taylor frowned. "I realize that, but I do need to at least try to do some research myself, you know. Otherwise, my employers will think I'm treating this trip like a vacation!" He laughed nervously.

Gina sighed. "Go ahead, then."

Jody couldn't stop herself. "You will be careful, won't you, Dr. Taylor?"

Dr. Taylor sighed impatiently. He didn't look at her. "I have been assured . . . er, Jody . . . that the firing of the dart will cause only the slightest discomfort to the animal," he said. "In fact, it may not feel anything at all, since I intend to put it into the fin, which is made of cartilage." He set his bag down on the deck and reached inside.

"Why don't you go below, Jody?" said Gina gently.

Jody bit her lip and shook her head. She was determined to stay and see what happened with her own eyes. She wanted to know if a dolphin was hurt or frightened by what Dr. Taylor did.

Finding the gun, Dr. Taylor checked it. Then, steadying his elbow against the side, he took careful aim and fired. The gun made a sharp, snapping sound and then a high whine as the dart shot out.

The dolphins responded immediately, disappearing beneath the water, the entire group moving as one. From the hydrophone amplifier came the sound of rapid, high-pitched chattering — as if, thought Jody, the dolphins were all exclaiming and asking one another what had just happened.

"I couldn't see whether or not you hit one," said Craig.

"Neither could I, but I'll tell you in a minute," said Dr. Taylor. He bent down again, creaking like one of the dolphins, and replaced the gun in his bag. Then he took out something that looked like a palm-sized computer. He pressed a couple of keys, checked the display, pressed again, and nodded, satisfied. "Bingo."

Jody could still hear the clicks and squeaks coming from the hydrophone, so — although she couldn't see them — she knew the dolphins must be near, as the hydrophone's range wasn't very wide. She leaned over the side and gazed down into the water.

Deep in the blue, there was a shadowy shape . . . two . . . three . . . six! Jody broke into a grin. Below the water, the dolphins were still following the boat; one or two lazily kept pace, while others shot forward, flipped over, and came back to swap places. Eventually, in five or ten minutes, they would have to come up for air, but they were in no hurry.

"What do you see?" asked Gina, leaning close. "Ah," she said. "I guess he didn't scare them off. The water certainly is clear today. And it doesn't seem as deep here. I wonder . . ."

Jody turned to look at her. "What are you thinking?"

Gina smiled. "What do you think I'm thinking?"

"I know what *I'm* thinking: that this would be a great place to dive!" Jody exclaimed happily.

"You could be right." Her mother nodded, returning her smile, then examined the brilliantly blue water again. "It looks to me like we might be getting close to the Florida Reef. It's the only living coral reef in the United States and it's what makes the water off the Keys such a paradise for divers. I'll go and check the navigation charts just to be sure, and I'll have a word with your father and Harry."

A few minutes later, Harry was giving orders to heave to, and Jody hurried below to change.

Brittany was in their cabin, painting her nails dark purple. She stared at Jody. "Are you actually going into the water with a whole *herd* of those animals?"

"If they stick around, I am," Jody replied.

"You must be crazy," Brittany said flatly. "I can't believe your mother is going to let you do that. After what she said . . ."

"What? What did she say?" Jody was bewildered.

"I overheard her warning you a while ago. She said that dolphins were wild animals and you couldn't trust them. She said there had been accidents, and people had gotten hurt." Brittany tossed her wavy hair back from her face and stared accusingly at Jody.

"Yes, *accidents*," Jody stressed. "Dolphins don't hurt

people, not normally. It's people who hurt dolphins. And I guess sometimes if people get too rough with them, then the dolphin might feel threatened and get rough back to defend itself. Mom just meant that you have to respect wild animals. Don't do things they might misunderstand. Let them come to you, if they want. You can't force them."

Brittany looked down and blew on her nails. "Oh! So it was, like, really smart of you to make that dolphin give you a ride."

Jody's jaw dropped. "I didn't *make* Apollo do anything, Brittany! It was all his idea."

"Sure." Brittany smirked in a self-satisfied way.

Jody opened her mouth to argue, but then she stopped. She couldn't force Brittany to believe her. She shrugged. "Have it your way."

On deck, Jody and her parents discussed their dive plan. She was glad to see the dolphins were still hanging around the boat.

"They may head for the hills when they see us coming — scary-looking critters that we are, with our tanks and regulators and fins!" Craig warned jokingly.

Jody nodded, but she had a feeling the dolphins would stick around out of curiosity. Dolphins seemed utterly fearless creatures to her. They would even head-butt sharks! It was only human beings who had ever posed a threat to dolphins, and yet, despite years of being captured, hurt, or killed, dolphins went on trying to make friends with people.

Craig insisted it was his turn to use the camera. "I'm sure our viewers would rather see two lovely mermaids than watch me flopping around."

"I wasn't planning on having you on camera, darling," his wife said dryly. "And our sponsors won't appreciate it if you produce a home video of your wife and daughter. I don't even want it switched on unless you're pointing it at a dolphin."

Jody went through the drill carefully with her parents: checking her tank and regulators; running through the few simple hand signals they would use to communicate underwater, indicating if there were any problems or that it was time to return.

She felt extra alert, excited by the prospect of entering the dolphins' territory on their terms. Although it had been wonderful to swim with Apollo, without scuba equipment she hadn't been able to dive very deeply, or stay underwater for more than a couple of minutes. This time, although she knew she would still be weak, slow, and clumsy in comparison with the dolphins, at least she would be able to stay in the dolphins' underwater world longer, and start to understand them better.

"Do you dive, Dr. Taylor?" Gina asked.

"I'm afraid I can't," he replied. He pointed to his head. "Trouble with my ears, you see."

He didn't sound sorry, Jody thought. She wondered if he even *liked* dolphins. But she had better things to think about. It was time to dive.

The dolphins moved away from the boat as Jody and her parents entered the water, but they did not go far. They were obviously curious about these visitors. They hung in the water, barely moving . . . just watching.

Clearing her ears, Jody sank down through the clear

blue water. She added some air to her buoyancy vest and her descent slowed. She hovered, trying to imitate the dolphins' posture and to keep as still as they did. It made her think of some silly game where the first one to move was "out."

Suddenly, one of the dolphins darted forward. It shot straight toward her. Jody tensed, half expecting a collision, but the dolphin came to a halt right in front of her. Its beak was just inches from her mask.

The friendly bottle-nosed face seemed to smile at Jody. She noticed the stream of silvery bubbles rising from the blowhole on the top of its head. After a few seconds the dolphin dropped a little lower in the water to circle her. The beak came questing forward, but never actually touched her. Then, with a push of its flippers, the dolphin moved away.

Jody decided to go after it, kicking with her own rubber fins. But even though the curious dolphin had seemed to be moving very slowly, she couldn't catch up with him.

As soon as Jody gave up the chase, two other dolphins appeared — one on either side of her. They kept pace with her, slowing when she slowed, but keeping just out of her reach. They were playing some kind of game, she decided.

Jody moved toward the dolphin on her right. He immediately moved away — out of reach, but only just — keeping the same distance between them. And at the

Me and my bodyguards

same time that Jody pulled away, the dolphin on her left moved toward her. It was almost like a dance!

The thought gave her an idea. She began to swim in a zigzag pattern. The two dolphins copied her. She went up and down as well as from side to side, trying all sorts of different movements. Although she couldn't watch them that well, she was pretty sure that they were both keeping up with her crazy routines.

Jody looked around for her mother and saw that she was hovering in the water not far away, face-to-face with the smallest dolphin. She noticed that bubbles were coming out of that dolphin's blowhole, too, and she wondered if the dolphins were imitating the rising stream of bubbles that accompanied all scuba divers. Then she caught a glimpse of her father swimming along on his side, pointing the video camera in its bright yellow waterproof shell.

And now, for your entertainment: Jody McGrath and the Dancing Dolphin Duo! she thought, waving to him and pointing at herself. Then she swam lower, toward the seabed.

The other two dolphins suddenly appeared out of

nowhere right in front of her. One of them shot down to the ocean floor, rooted around in the sand with its nose, and then emerged with a prize in its jaws: a starfish!

This seemed to be the signal for a new game. Excited clicking and chattering noises came from all around. Jody's dancing partners abandoned her and rushed toward the one with the starfish. But it shot away and the others chased it.

Jody could only stare after them, wishing she could play, too. But she didn't have the speed for this game.

Four dolphins all ganged up on the one with the starfish. For a few moments there were five tumbling, whirling bodies in a cloud of bubbles. Then the turmoil broke up. One of the dolphins streaked away, coming back toward Jody.

She saw that this one — she couldn't tell if it was the same or a different one — carried the starfish. It swam above her — she saw the paler belly — and then it suddenly swooped down and dropped the starfish.

The starfish drifted down through the water until Jody stopped its progress by catching it in her hand.

What now? she wondered. They were all watching her, waiting for something. What was she supposed to do? She didn't like the idea of trying to outswim them with it, and being mobbed by all six dolphins. But it was useless trying to throw it for them; it would go no distance before drifting toward the bottom.

Then one of the dolphins moved away from the others and swam toward her. It swam very close, on a level with her hands, close enough for her to touch — and then it opened its mouth.

Jody stared at the regular, triangular teeth that lined its jaws. Then, very carefully, she placed the starfish between them.

The dolphin gave a series of rapid clicks as he closed his mouth gently on the starfish. Then he flipped over on his back and shot rapidly away, with his friends in noisy pursuit. This time, they all rose upward, giving Jody a unique, dolphin's-eye view of their activities.

Jody kicked off from the bottom and swam upward, wanting to join them. But she was too slow. It was like a baby trying to join in a football game, she thought. Humans could play with dolphins only when the dolphins were willing to make the game slow, simple, and gentle enough for the land-living creatures to keep up. But as she trailed after them, Jody thought she was incredibly lucky to be allowed to come so close to these wonderful, graceful creatures in the sea.

All too soon, she saw her mother's signal to return to the surface. Playtime was over.

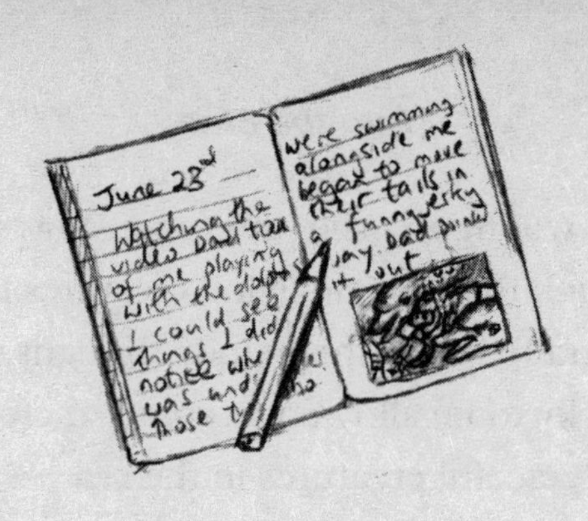

9

June 23 — bedtime.

Watching the video Dad took of me playing with the dolphins, I could see things I didn't notice when I was underwater. Those two that were swimming alongside me began to move their tails in a funny, jerky way. Dad pointed it out. He said maybe they weren't just keeping pace with me, but were trying to imitate the way I swam. Were they making fun of me? Dad said no, probably they were trying to understand what it felt like to be me — just like I try to imagine sometimes, when I'm swimming underwater, that I'm a dolphin.

I decided to give them all names. Maddie suggested we stick with the Greek myths for inspiration. So, the one that reminds me the most of Apollo is Artemis, since she was Apollo's twin sister in the legends. The biggest one — Dad thinks he must be around three and a half yards long, and he's the most powerful-looking in the group — is Poseidon. Poseidon was the god of the sea, and the dolphin was sacred to him. Poseidon had a son called Triton, so that's what I've named the smallest dolphin in the group. The one carrying the micro-transmitter in his fin (you can see a piece of bright blue plastic sticking out) is Hermes, because he was the messenger of the gods. Our Hermes will carry messages about where the group is in relation to us.

Then I was stumped and couldn't think of names for the last two. They look absolutely identical and don't have any markings to suggest special names. Sean said they were twin dolphins, and weren't there some famous twins in Greek mythology? So those two are Castor and Pollux, the Gemini twins.

Poseidon, Triton, Hermes, Artemis, Castor, and Pollux have all disappeared, but we know from Dr. Taylor's transmitter that they are only two or three miles away — or maybe more now, or less. They don't stay in one spot for long but are always on the move. Even when they sleep they only "catnap" for a short while, resting near the surface. According to Mom, some researchers think that dolphins sleep with only half of their brain at a time!

Still no sign of Apollo. I can't help thinking he'd be happier if he were part of a group like the one we saw today.

First thing the next morning, as usual, Jody ran out onto the deck to look for dolphins.

Maddie stopped her as she passed, to give her a flask of freshly brewed coffee. "Could you take this up to Cam?"

Cam, who had spent the past two hours on watch-duty, looked pleased to see her, even though Jody suspected he would rather have had a visit from Maddie.

Jody looked around. The sea looked very gray today, beneath a heavy, overcast sky, and the air was warm and humid. She stared out at the horizon and saw a line of pelicans flapping low above the water. Something splashed nearby, but when she quickly turned to look, she could see nothing.

"Flying fish," Cam said. "They're really jumping. One of 'em slapped me in the face a little while ago — wham! What a way to start the day."

Jody giggled. "Have you seen any dolphins?"

Cam widened his green eyes at her. "Would I see a dolphin and not tell you?"

"I don't know." Jody felt embarrassed.

"Of course I wouldn't," he said easily. He winked. "Don't worry, you'll hear from me if I spot so much as a single fin of any . . .what are they called again?" he asked teasingly. "Oh, yeah — cetaceans."

"Thanks," Jody replied.

"Don't mention it." He took a careful sip of the coffee and sighed with pleasure. "Hey, Jody — if there're any biscuits for breakfast, could you ask someone to bring me one?"

She nodded. The mention of breakfast reminded her that she was hungry — and delicious smells were rising from the galley. After a final, wistful gaze out to sea, Jody went below to eat.

June 24 — after breakfast.

I almost wish I'd let Dr. Taylor put the transmitter into Apollo. Hermes didn't seem to mind it, and Dr. Taylor said it will drop out, anyway, in a few weeks. I would feel happier if I knew where Apollo was.

But that's silly. Apollo is at home in the ocean, whether or not I know where he is. Probably he has gone back to his group, or joined up with a new one. Dolphins are social animals, but Mom says they belong to different groups at different times; they aren't members of the same pod all their lives, like whales.

But I can't stop thinking that Apollo was lonely. I wish I could know that he was all right, after all.

The soft sound of something bumping the hull of the boat made Jody pause and look up. It hadn't sounded like the slap of a wave. As she strained her ears, she was rewarded with the faint but unmistakable sound of a dolphin's whistle.

Her heart gave a thump. She dropped her pencil, jumped out of her bunk, and hurried out on deck, with only one thought in her mind. She hardly noticed that someone called out to her as she raced past.

Up in the open air, Jody saw the familiar dolphin shape in the water right away. She scanned the waves searching for the rest of the group. But this dolphin was alone.

"Apollo?" Jody clutched the rail and leaned out over the side. The wind pushed back her hair and stroked her cheeks.

Below, the dolphin rose up, whistling. It seemed a familiar sound, or was she kidding herself? Yet it was certainly doing its best to attract her attention, Jody thought. His interest in her had to be more than just curiosity. She was *almost* sure it was Apollo.

Then the dolphin turned slightly and leaped up, presenting its right side to her. There was the curving, harp-shaped mark she remembered! It *was* Apollo — without any doubt.

Jody felt she would burst with happiness and excitement! She wanted to run and tell everyone the good news, but she didn't want to leave her newfound friend even for a minute. Luckily, her mother turned up within a few moments, looking puzzled.

"What's going on? The way you raced out, I thought it must be . . ." Her voice trailed off as she saw the dolphin beside the boat. She sighed and shook her head. "I should have known! You and dolphins . . ." Then she looked even more puzzled. "But how on earth did you know? Have you developed psychic powers all of a sudden?"

Jody laughed and shook her head. "I heard something — a little bump against the side of the boat — and I thought I'd come out to check. But oh, Mom, don't you see? It's *Apollo*! He's come back!"

Gina raised her eyebrows, looking skeptical. "Sure that's not just wishful thinking? One bottle-nosed dolphin looks a lot like any other."

Jody pointed at the leaping, racing animal beside the boat. "But look at him! He's excited to see me again. A strange dolphin wouldn't be acting like that, would he?"

Gina thought about it. She walked closer to the side,

grasped the metal railing, and leaned over. For a long minute she gazed into the water and listened.

When she turned back to her daughter, her face was thoughtful. "You're right," she said. "He *is* excited. Those noises he's making . . . well, I wouldn't want to swear to it, I'd really want to be able to listen to the tape again and not rely on my memory, but it does remind me . . ."

"Remind you of what?" Jody demanded, ready to burst with impatience.

"A few years ago I did some work with a couple of captive dolphins known as George and Martha," her mother explained. "Martha was sent away for a while, and George was very unhappy without her. She was brought back, but before George had seen her, before she was returned to the tank, he began this excited vocalizing. It was as if somehow he already knew she had returned." Gina smiled at Jody. "Maybe Apollo's just happy to see you," she said lightly.

Jody frowned. Apollo might be happy to see her, but that wasn't the whole story. She remembered the way the other dolphins had bumped against the boat . . . and she had an idea. "Do dolphins have a good sense of smell?" she asked.

"No," Gina replied, sounding surprised. "They probably can't smell at all. Certainly not the way land animals do."

"Oh," said Jody, disappointed. She had thought about the way dogs know if other dogs have been nearby, and she had wondered if Apollo could possibly have picked up some traces that would tell him other dolphins — maybe his friends? — had been around *Dolphin Dreamer* recently. But now she realized that smelling anything underwater was pretty unlikely.

But Gina went on. "They certainly have a sense of taste, and that probably makes up for the lack of smell. Studies have shown that they can sense even very tiny amounts of chemicals in water, and tell the difference between them."

Jody remembered that the dolphins' skin produced an oil to help them glide through the water. She wondered if any of that oil might still be on the side of the boat where the other dolphins had bumped it the day before. Was it possible that Apollo could taste the oil and recognize that it came from one of his friends? He might be desperately asking her where they'd gone . . . if only she could tell him.

"Jody? What's on your mind?" Gina asked, looking puzzled.

Jody was just about to explain when she had a brilliant idea. She caught her breath. "Mom, where's Dr. Taylor?"

"I don't know," her mother replied, looking even more puzzled. "Probably in his cabin. Why? Jody, what's going on?"

"I've got to talk to him. It's really important!" Jody cried. Then she began to scramble down the hatch. She didn't want to waste any more time. It was important to act quickly, before Apollo left again. She had to find out if her idea would work.

Jody found Dr. Jefferson Taylor relaxing in the main cabin, sipping from a tall glass of iced tea while he paged through a magazine for coin collectors. He wore a faded navy-blue T-shirt, which was stretched a little too tightly across his bulging middle, and his baggy shorts revealed hairy, knobby knees.

"Dr. Taylor," she cried excitedly. "I want to talk to you!"

"You do? Why?" Dr. Taylor clutched his magazine and peered nervously over it, as if expecting trouble.

Jody took a deep breath. "I wanted to ask if you could still track down that group of dolphins."

Dr. Taylor looked surprised at Jody's interest after her earlier disapproval. "The one I tagged yesterday? Yes, of course," he replied. "They can't possibly have traveled out of range yet. In fact, I was just about to check their whereabouts." He laid the magazine aside and stood up.

"*Great!*" Jody cried. She thought quickly. "Dr. Taylor, do you think, when you use your equipment to track them down, you could mark their position on the navigation chart? Then Harry could sail there. You'd have to keep tracking, since dolphins don't stay in one spot for long. But we could — "

"Jody, what are you trying to set up?" It was her father's voice. Jody turned to see both her parents staring at her in some bewilderment. Brittany was standing there, too, her face hard and malicious.

"Isn't it obvious?" Brittany spoke up, before Jody had a chance to answer. "She thinks this is *her* expedition. You guys should hear the junk she tells me about how much she knows, how Dolphin Universe was all her idea, and about all the work she's done to make it happen. She thinks she knows everything. Now she's decided that she's the boss! My dad won't go where I want, but if *Jody* asks him to change course, he'll hop right to it."

Jody was stunned by the hate-filled words pouring out of Brittany. Surely her parents couldn't believe what Brittany was saying. She looked desperately at their faces as they listened.

Gina turned to her daughter, her expression serious. "Okay, Brittany, let's hear Jody's side of the story. Well, Jody?"

"It's not true," Jody said hotly.

"Then maybe you should tell us exactly what did happen," said Craig gently. His normally easygoing face was unusually serious.

Jody felt close to tears. Everything was going horribly wrong. Nobody understood her. "I'm not trying to run things myself, honest," she said in a choked voice. "But I had this idea . . . and, well, I just wanted to know if what I thought of doing was *possible* before I asked you about it. But I *was* going to ask, just as soon as I worked it out." Her voice trailed away. She felt like a burst balloon.

"Well, why don't you tell us all now?" said Craig. He still looked serious, but it was clear he wasn't angry at her.

Everyone crowded around the table to listen — except Brittany, who hung back, trying to look as if she wasn't interested.

Jody explained her theory that Apollo might have "tasted" the presence of the other dolphins, and that was why he'd been so excited to find their boat again. Then she told them her idea: that they should track down the dolphin group and lead Apollo to them. She looked anxiously at her parents to see what they thought.

"You know," said Craig gently, "if Apollo has been separated from his group, chances are he'll soon find them again. Dolphins are much better at tracking things in the ocean than we humans are, even with our fancy equipment. And Poseidon and Company may not have anything to do with your Apollo."

"I know, I thought of that," Jody said quickly. "But even if they weren't his group to begin with, you did say that dolphins migrate to different groups sometimes. Maybe something happened to his old group and he needs a new one. I'm sure he doesn't want to be all alone. I want to give him a chance to meet some other dolphins."

Her parents exchanged a glance.

Jody held her breath.

Then Craig smiled. "Well, why not? Maybe it will turn out to be a wild-dolphin chase — but that's what we're here for, to follow wild dolphins. And it will give Dr. Taylor a chance to use his equipment."

Dr. Taylor brightened up at that. "Certainly, and I'll be happy to demonstrate it to you," he said.

"Yes, I'm sure you would," Craig said hastily. "But we might be a little busy for a long and scientific explanation."

Jody saw her mother's mouth twitch with amusement, and she guessed she was thinking about the long and boring message for TV that Dr. Taylor had recorded a few days earlier.

"All right, then," said Craig. "Let's get started. If you can locate the dolphin, Dr. Taylor, Harry and I can plot a new course."

As everyone rose from the table, Craig stopped and wagged his finger at Jody. "I like it when my kids have brilliant ideas," he said. "But, in the future, would you please run them by me or your mother before involving anybody else?"

"I will," Jody agreed. She tried to sound meek, but somehow a grin insisted on spreading across her face. Her dad thought it was a brilliant idea!

However, a few minutes later, as she hung over the side of the boat and watched Apollo keeping pace with them, she couldn't help thinking of all the many things that could go wrong with her plan. Apollo might lose interest in following them at any minute. Or they might not be able to catch up to the dolphins, even by sailing all day. Dolphins could speed through the water much faster than *Dolphin Dreamer*. They might keep them traveling in circles until Harry got fed up and refused to continue. Or, if Apollo didn't abandon them and they did find the other dolphins, maybe Poseidon and the others wouldn't like Apollo. They might even drive him away. One theory that Jody had read about lone dolphins who made friends with people was that they were outcasts from their groups.

But, like her mother, Jody believed it was best to think positive. And, since they might be sailing for hours yet, it made sense to try not to worry.

That afternoon, Jody sat on the foredeck, watching Apollo. He seemed to be having a great time, bow-riding. He had disappeared occasionally as they traveled, but never for very long. Jody couldn't help feeling that Apollo sensed there was a special reason to stay with *Dolphin Dreamer* and that he shared the excitement that kept bubbling up inside her.

Jody gazed out to sea. The clouds had burned away and the sky was a hard, clear blue overhead. Freshening winds blew them along rapidly — by good luck, in exactly the direction they wanted to go.

Suddenly, Jody froze, clutching the rail hard with excitement. Was that a dorsal fin rising above the waves? Was that another dolphin out there? Yes, it was! And another . . . and another! She gave a yell of triumph and called, "Dolphins off the starboard bow!"

She glanced down at the lower deck and saw that her parents were ready with the camera, and Harry was bringing the boat about, slowing their speed as they approached the dolphins. She looked back down at Apollo — and caught her breath. He'd disappeared.

Then, as Jody searched the water with anxious eyes, she saw him. Apollo was swimming beneath the water, his body like a sleek, gray bullet, heading straight for the other dolphins. She sighed with relief. Of course,

Apollo must have sensed the other dolphins, must have heard their songs, way before she saw them.

The others — Poseidon, Triton, Artemis, Hermes, Castor, and Pollux — formed a tight group and hovered in a mass in the water, unmoving as they waited for Apollo. They didn't look very friendly, and Jody felt a clutch of anxiety. Had she done the right thing? Was Apollo going to be all right?

All of a sudden, as if Apollo had crossed some invisible line in the water, the herd stopped waiting, and charged at him. Big Poseidon was in the lead, and Jody saw him hit Apollo broadside. She saw the impact make Apollo spin away, and she covered her mouth in horror. Poor Apollo! What had she done?

But Apollo recovered quickly and charged back through the water at Poseidon, slamming against the bigger dolphin. Then, twisting away, Apollo swam rapidly to the center of the group, and suddenly they were all slamming against one another, spinning, diving down, and leaping up in the air.

Jody breathed out with relief as she finally under-

Good-bye, Apollo!

stood. They were playing! Now, as they leaped and dived, together and apart, it was impossible to mistake this behavior for anything other than having fun!

Apollo wasn't on his own anymore.

June 24 — continued.

Apollo is back where he belongs — with his friends. Maybe he'd always known where they were; probably he would have found his way back to them in another day or two, without the help of Dolphin Dreamer. *But I'm glad we were there to see the reunion. It was a wonderful sight to see.*

And to think that this is only the beginning of our great adventure!

Thanks to the Whale and Dolphin Conservation Society for reviewing the dolphin information contained in this book.

You will find lots more about dolphins on these websites:

The Whale and Dolphin Conservation Society
www.wdcs.org
International Dolphin Watch **www.idw.org**